GAVRIIL TROYEPOLSKY

BEEM

Translated from the Russian
by Antonina W. Bouis

HARPER & ROW, PUBLISHERS

New York Hagerstown San Francisco London

This work was first published in Russian under the title *Belyi Beem Chernoe Ukho,* © 1971 Gauriil Troyepolsky.

BEEM. English translation copyright © 1978 by Harper & Row, Publishers, Inc. All rights reserved. Printed in the United States of America. No part of this book may be used or reproduced in any manner whatsoever without written permission except in the case of brief quotations embodied in critical articles and reviews. For information address Harper & Row, Publishers, Inc., 10 East 53rd Street, New York, N.Y. 10022. Published simultaneously in Canada by Fitzhenry & Whiteside Limited, Toronto.

FIRST EDITION

Designed by C. Linda Dingler

Library of Congress Cataloging in Publication Data

Troepol'skii, Gavriil Nikolaevich, 1905–
    Beem

    1. Dogs—Legends and stories. I.–Title.
PZ4.T845Be [PG3476.T74]   891.7′3′44   78–2072
ISBN 0–06–014348–7

78 79 80 81 82 10 9 8 7 6 5 4 3 2 1

To Alexander Trifonovich Tvardovsky

1

TWO IN A ROOM

Pitifully and, it seemed, hopelessly, he would begin to whine, rolling clumsily from side to side—looking for his mother. Then his master would take him on his lap and give him milk in a baby bottle.

And what else was a month-old puppy to do when he still understood absolutely nothing about life and his mother didn't come despite all his complaints? He performed his sad little concerts during those first two days. But he always ended up asleep in his master's arms, cuddling his bottle.

By the fourth day, the tiny creature was used to the warmth of human hands. Puppies respond very quickly to tenderness.

He didn't know his own name yet, but by week's end he had definitely established that he was Beem.

At two months, he was surprised to see objects: a desk towering high above him, and on the wall, a gun, a game bag, and the face of a person with long hair. He got used to it all very quickly. There was nothing amazing in the fact that the figure on the wall was motionless—but it wasn't interesting because it didn't move. Of course, later on, Beem would take quick looks at it just to see what it could mean—a face peering out of a frame like a window.

The other wall was much more entertaining. It was made up of different blocks that his master could take out and replace at will. At four months, when Beem could reach them by standing on his hind legs, he pulled one out himself and tried to examine it. But for some reason it rustled and left a piece of paper in Beem's mouth. It was great fun to tear that piece apart into tiny bits.

"What's this?" his master yelled. "No!" And he rubbed Beem's nose in the book. "No, Beem. No!"

That kind of suggestion would be enough to make even a man give up reading, but not Beem; he watched the books closely for a long time, cocking his head to one side and then the other. And apparently he came to the following decision: If I can't touch that one, I'll try this one. He quietly latched onto the spine and dragged the book under the couch; there he chewed off one corner of the cover and then another, and then, forgetting, he pulled the book out into the middle of the room and mauled it playfully with his paws, pouncing on it.

And that was the moment when he learned what "pain" and "no" really meant.

His master got up from the table and said sternly: "No!" And he pulled Beem's ear. "You stupid dog, you've ripped up my *Bible for Believers and Nonbelievers.*" And then again: "No! Don't touch books!" And he pulled Beem's ear once more.

Beem squealed and raised all four paws in the air. Lying on his back, he looked at his master and couldn't understand what was going on.

"No! No!" his master persisted, shoving the book into Beem's nose again and again, but not punishing him anymore. Then he picked up the puppy, petted him, and repeated, "No, little baby. No, silly little puppy." And he sat down. And put Beem on his lap.

And so, at an early age, Beem learned a lesson from his master through *The Bible for Believers and Nonbelievers.* Beem licked his master's hand and peered into his face.

He already enjoyed it when his master talked to him, even

2

though he knew only two words as yet: "Beem" and "no." But it was so interesting to watch the white hair fall across the forehead and the kind lips move, and to feel the warm, gentle fingers on his fur. Beem could tell for sure whether his master was happy or sad, scolding him or praising him, calling or chasing him away.

There were times when he was sad. Then he would talk to himself but address Beem: "So that's our life, silly. What are you staring at her for?" He meant the portrait. "She's dead, fellow. Gone, she's gone." He would pet Beem and add with complete confidence, "You're my silly little dummy, Beem. You don't understand a thing yet."

But he was only partially right, because Beem did understand that his master wouldn't play with him just then, and he knew that the words "silly" and "little boy" were meant for him. So whenever his big friend called him "silly" or "little boy," Beem would come right away, as though it were his name. And if he could understand a tone of voice at such an early age, then of course he promised to be a marvelously wise dog.

But is intelligence alone enough to determine a dog's standing among his brethren? Unfortunately, no. His mental capacities aside, not everything was right with Beem.

Of course, his parents were both thoroughbred setters, with long pedigrees. Each parent had papers. Using those papers, his master could have found out Beem's great-grandparents, and even their great-grandparents if he had wanted to. That was all very fine. But Beem, with all his good qualities, had one great defect, which later had a profound influence on his fate: even though he was a Gordon setter, his coloring was all wrong, completely atypical. According to the official standards for hunting dogs, a Gordon setter has to be "black, with a shiny bluish sheen—like a raven's wing—and with clearly defined tan flank markings." Even white markings in unacceptable places are considered terrible flaws in Gordon setters. Beem was born

3

with a white body and rust-colored markings and spots; only one ear and one leg were black, raven-black at that; his other ear was pale tan. It was really amazing: here was a purebred Gordon setter, but his coloring had nothing to do with the breed. Some distant ancestor showed up in Beem; he was an albino.

In general, his multicolored ears and the markings under his big, wise, dark-brown eyes made Beem's face even more appealing, memorable, and wiser, or more philosophical and meditative than an ordinary dog's. He seemed really to have a doggy human face. But in dog-breeding circles his white coloring indicated degeneration. Although he was a beauty in every way, according to the official standard he was dubious and even flawed. And that was Beem's problem.

Of course, Beem had no idea of this flaw; even puppies cannot choose their ancestors. He simply gave the matter no thought. He just lived and enjoyed life for the time being.

But his master worried: Would Beem get his papers, which would guarantee his rank among hunting dogs, or would he remain an outcast all his life? That would be decided only when he was six months old, when the puppy would (again according to dog-breeding rules) be old enough to be classified as a pedigreed dog.

The owner of Beem's mother had already decided to get rid of the white pup—that is, to drown him—but an eccentric had come along who pitied the strange pup. That eccentric was now Beem's master. He had liked Beem's eyes; he thought they were wise. And now he faced the question: Would Beem get his papers or not? And tried to figure out how such an anomaly could have occurred. He went through all the books on hunting and dog breeding to get a little closer to the truth so as to prove it wasn't Beem's fault. And he began copying into a thick notebook anything from the books that might substantiate Beem's claim to being a real representative of the Gordon setter breed.

4

Beem was his friend by now, and you always have to help your friends. Otherwise, Beem would not be in the winner's circle at dog shows, and gold medals wouldn't jangle on his chest. No matter how good he was at hunting, he would be excluded from the circle of pedigreed dogs forever.

How unfair life can be!

From His Master's Notes

In the last months, Beem has crept into my heart unnoticed and taken up permanent residence. How did he do it? With his kindness, boundless trust, and gentleness—an irresistible combination as long as there is no fawning mixed in, because fawning can in time turn all the other feelings—kindness, and trust, and gentleness—into false ones. It's a terrible quality. Spare us! Heaven forbid! But for now, Beem is a baby and a sweet dog. How he turns out will depend on me, his master.

Strange, but I've been noticing something new about me. For instance, if I come across a picture with a dog in it, the first thing I look at is the dog's coloring and breed. My anxiety over Beem's certification is showing.

A few days ago at the museum, I noticed Jacopo da Bassano's painting *Moses Smites Water from the Rock* (sixteenth century). There is a dog in the foreground—an obvious prototype of the setter, but with strange markings: the body is white, the face, divided by a white streak, is black, the ears are *also black,* the nose is white, there is a black spot on the left shoulder, and the flank is also black. Exhausted and emaciated, the dog is drinking greedily from a bowl.

Another dog, with long hair, also has *black ears.* Weakened by thirst, it rests its head on its master's lap and waits patiently for the water. Nearby are a rabbit and a rooster, and there are two lambs on the left.

5

What was the artist trying to say by placing the dogs in the foreground with the people? Apparently, that people loved dogs even in antiquity and never abandoned them, even in times of disaster, even when an entire people were on the brink of extinction, and that dogs remained loyal and faithful, ready to die alongside man.

For, just a minute earlier, they had been desperate, without a shred of hope. And they had been looking Moses in the eye and saying to Moses, who had led them out of slavery, "Would to God we had died by the hand of God in the land of Egypt, when we sat by the fleshpots and we did eat bread to the full! For ye have brought us forth into the wilderness to kill this whole assembly with hunger."

Moses realized with great bitterness just how strongly the spirit of servility was ingrained in the people: all the bread they could eat and kettles of meat were worth more to them than freedom. And so he smote water from the cliff. And then it was good for all who followed him, and that was what Bassano revealed in his painting.

Perhaps the painter put the dogs in the foreground as a rebuke to people for their own weakness in adversity, as a symbol of fidelity, hope, and loyalty? Anything is possible. It was a long time ago.

Bassano's painting is over three hundred years old. Could the black-and-white markings in Beem come from those days? Impossible. But nature is nature.

Still, I doubt that it could mitigate the objections to Beem and the anomalous markings on his body and ears. For the more ancient the examples, the stronger the case will be that he's a throwback and unworthy of a pedigree.

No, I must look for something else. And if one of the experts should mention the Bassano painting to me, I'll just say, "What do black ears in Bassano have to do with it?"

6

Let's look for data a little closer in time to Beem.

An excerpt from a book on standards for gun dogs:

Gordon setters were bred in Scotland. . . . The breed developed by the *middle of the 19th century*. . . . Modern Scottish setters, while maintaining their strength and massive bone structure, have acquired greater speed. The dogs have a calm, even temper, are obedient and gentle, and take to their work early and well, and can be worked successfully in swamps and in the woods. . . . Their characteristic pointing stance is distinctive, steady, and high, with the head no lower than the nape.

From the two-volume *Dogs* by L. P. Sabaneyev, author of the marvelous books *Hunting Calendar* and *Fish of Russia:*

If we take into account the fact that the origins of the setter lie in the oldest race of hunting dogs, which was domesticated over the course of many centuries, then we will not be surprised that setters are probably the most cultured and intelligent breed.

There! That means that Beem comes from an intelligent breed. That could come in handy.

From the same book by Sabaneyev:

In 1847 Perland brought as a gift for Grand Duke Mikhail Pavlovich two marvelously beautiful and very rare setters. . . . The dogs were not for sale and were traded for a horse valued at 2,000 rubles.

There. He brought them as a gift, yet he fleeced the Grand Duke for a sum that could have bought twenty serfs. But were the dogs at fault? And what does Beem have to do with it? This won't do.

From a letter from S. V. Pensky, well-known naturalist, hunter, and dog breeder in his day, to L. P. Sabaneyev:

During the Crimean War, I saw a beautiful red setter at Sukhovo-Kobylin's, the author of *Krechinsky's Wedding,* and some dappled ones in Ryazan at the house of the artist Pyotr Sokolov.

Aha, this is more to the point. How interesting—even the satirist had a setter then. And the artist had kept tan dappled ones. Is that where your bloodline comes from, Beem? Wouldn't that be wonderful! But then, what about the black ear? I don't understand.

From the same letter:

Bers, the court physician in Moscow, also bred red setters. He mated one of the red bitches with a black setter that had belonged to the late Emperor Alexander. I don't know what the pups looked like or what happened to them, but I do know that Count Leo Tolstoy raised one of them at his estate.

Stop! Could this be it? If your black leg and ear come from a dog that belonged to Leo Tolstoy, you are a lucky dog, Beem, even without a certificate of pedigree, the luckiest dog of all the dogs in the world. The great writer loved dogs.

More from that letter:

I saw the Emperor's black setter in Ilyinsky after a supper the Tsar gave for the members of the Moscow Hunt Society. It was a very large and totally beautiful indoor dog, with a marvelous head and fine coat, but with little resembling the setter type about it; its legs were too long, and one of them was *completely white*. They say that the setter was a gift of some Polish lord, and there was a rumor that it wasn't completely thoroughbred.

Does that mean that the Polish lord hoodwinked the Emperor? It's possible. That could happen on the canine front as well. What a pain that imperial black setter is! Of course, there's also the blood of Bers' tan bitch, that had an "extraordinarily keen sense of smell and marvelous pointing." That means that even if your leg comes from the Emperor's setter, Beem, it's still quite possible that you could be a distant descendant of the great writer's dog. But no, Beem, hush! Not a word about the Tsar's dog. It never happened—and that's all there is to it. That's all we need.

What is left for ammunition if it comes to an argument in Beem's defense?

Moses is out for obvious reasons. Sukhovo-Kobylin is out because of the time and the markings. That leaves Leo Tolstoy: 1) the closest in time; 2) the father of his dog was black and the mother red. It all fits. But the father, the black setter, belonged to the Tsar—that's the problem. I'll have to keep silent about my attempts to trace Beem's more distant relatives. Therefore the commission will base its decision only on the pedigree of Beem's mother and father, the way they usually do; there's no white dog in the line, and that's that. And Tolstoy would mean nothing to them. And they would be right. And really, anyone could trace back his dog to the great writer's dog, and then it's easy enough to find a blood tie to the writer Tolstoy himself. And so many Tolstoys have cropped up lately! There's a whole cloud of them darkening the horizon.

No matter how painful, I am prepared rationally to accept the fact that Beem will be an outcast from the world of pedigreed dogs. Too bad. Only one thing is left: Beem comes from an intelligent breed. But that is no proof (that's why they have standards).

"It's no good, Beem, no good," his master sighed, putting aside his pen and sticking the notebook in a drawer.

Beem, hearing his name, got up from his bed, sat up, cocked his head to the side of the black ear, as though he listened only with his tan one. And that was a very cozy trait. His whole being seemed to say, "You are a good man, my kind friend. I'm listening. What do you want?"

His master cheered up at Beem's question and said, "You're

a sweetheart, Beem! We'll live together, even without your certification. You're a good dog. Everyone loves a good dog." He put Beem on his lap and petted him, muttering, "It's all right. It'll be all right, anyway, little one."

Beem felt warm and cozy. And he learned a lesson for his whole life: "good" meant tenderness, gratitude, and friendship.

And Beem fell asleep. What did he care who his master was? The important thing was that he was kind and dear.

"Hey, black ear, imperial leg," the man said softly and put Beem back on his bed.

He stood before the window for a long time, staring into the deep-purple night. Then he looked over at the portrait of the woman and said, "You see, it's a little easier for me. I'm not alone anymore." He hadn't noticed that in his loneliness he had gradually come to talk aloud to "her" or to himself. Now he also talked to Beem. "I'm not alone anymore," he told the portrait.

Beem slept.

And so they lived together in their one room. Beem grew up strong and healthy. He quickly learned that his master's name was "Ivan Ivanovich." He was a smart pup; he caught on fast. And gradually he understood that he couldn't touch anything, he could just look at things and people. And in general, he couldn't do anything unless his master allowed him or ordered him to do it. And so the word "no" became Beem's guiding rule in life. And Ivan Ivanovich's eyes, tone of voice, gestures, clear words of command, and words of love determined the dog's life. Most important, under no circumstances could an independently chosen course of action go against his master's wishes. But Beem was beginning to guess at some of his friend's intentions. For example, Ivan Ivanovich would stand in front of the window and stare out into space and think hard. Then Beem would sit next to him and also stare and think. The man didn't know what the dog was thinking, but the dog's whole appear-

10

ance said, "Now my kind friend is going to sit down at the desk. He'll walk back and forth from one corner to the other, and then he'll sit down and move a stick across white paper, and the stick will rustle quietly. This will take a long time, so I'll sit with him and keep him company." Then he would nuzzle his master's warm hand with his nose.

And Ivan Ivanovich would say, "Well, little Beem, let's get to work." And he really would sit down.

And Beem would settle in a rolled-up ball at his feet, or, if he was told, "Go to your place," he would go back to his bed in the corner and wait. Wait for a look, a word, a gesture. Actually, after a while he could leave his bed and devote himself to the round bone that he couldn't chew up but which was good for his teeth—he could do that as long as he didn't disturb the man.

But when Ivan Ivanovich hid his face in his hands, leaning on the table, then Beem would come over and lay his head on his master's lap. And wait. He knew he'd be petted. He knew his friend was unhappy.

And Ivan Ivanovich would thank him: "Thanks, sweetie. Thanks, Beem." And then he'd rustle his stick on the white paper some more.

That's the way it was at home.

But it was different in the fields, where they both forgot everything. Beem could run, and play, and chase butterflies, roll in the grass—everything was allowed. But even here, after Beem was eight months old, his master's commands determined everything: "Go on, go!"—you can play; "Back!"—that's clear enough; "Lie down!"—that's absolutely clear; "Up!"—jump over; "Seek!"—look for the pieces of cheese; "Heel!"—walk alongside him, but only on the left; "Come here!"—back to his master quickly, and there'll be a piece of sugar. And Beem learned many other words before he was a year old. The friends understood each other more and more, loved each other, and lived as equals—man and dog.

11

Suddenly something happened that changed Beem's life, and he grew up in a few days. And it happened only because Beem discovered a major, amazing flaw in his master.

It happened this way. Beem was nuzzling his way along the meadow carefully and intently, looking for the scattered cheese, and suddenly, among the various scents of grasses, flowers, the soil, and the river, came a stream of air that was unusual and troubling; it smelled of a bird that did not resemble the ones Beem knew—sparrows, merry titmice, tailwags, and other small birds that were impossible to catch, so that there was no point in even trying. This was the smell of something unknown that made his blood course. Beem stopped and looked back at Ivan Ivanovich. Who turned aside without having noticed a thing. Beem was stunned; his friend couldn't smell. He was crippled! And Beem decided on his own; stalking quietly, he approached the unknown without a second look at Ivan Ivanovich. His steps became shorter and shorter; he seemed to be picking a spot for every paw so as not to rustle the grass or brush up against a single stalk. Finally the smell was so strong that he couldn't go any further. And Beem froze in place, his right foreleg suspended, as if turned to stone. He became a statue of a dog created by an exquisite sculptor. There it was, his first point! The first manifestation of a passion for the hunt to the point of oblivion.

Oh, no, his master came over quietly and petted Beem, who was trembling with excitement.

"Good, good, little one. Good." And he took him by the collar. "Forward . . . Forward . . ."

But Beem couldn't move. He didn't have the strength.

"Forward . . . Forward . . ." Ivan Ivanovich pulled him.

And Beem went! Slowly, very slowly. And he could tell, the unknown was close by. And suddenly the harsh command: "Forward!"

Beem raced ahead. The quail flew up noisily. Beem rushed

12

after it and—and—and—chased it, passionately, with all his might.

"Back!" called his master.

But Beem heard nothing, as if he had no ears.

"Back!" And a whistle. "Back!" And a whistle.

Beem ran on until he lost sight of the quail, and then, happy and joyous, he returned. But what was this? His master looked angry and stern and didn't pet him. It was obvious: his friend couldn't smell a thing! Poor, pathetic friend. Beem licked Ivan Ivanovich's hand gingerly, to express his pity for the astounding congenital flaw in the living creature closest to him in the world.

His master said, "You were all wrong, silly." And then, in a jollier tone, "Well, then, Beem, let's start in earnest." He took off Beem's collar and replaced it with another (uncomfortable) one and attached a long leash to it. "Seek!"

Now Beem searched for the quail scent—and nothing else. And Ivan Ivanovich directed him toward the place where the bird had alighted. Beem had no idea that his friend had seen the quail settle after the shameful chase (he couldn't smell, of course, but he could see).

And there was that scent! Beem, no longer noticing the leash, shortened his cast, sniffed, raised his head, and caught the scent high. Another point! Against the setting sun he was astounding in his beauty, which it is given very few men to appreciate.

Trembling with excitement himself, Ivan Ivanovich wrapped the end of the leash tightly around his hand and commanded softly, "Forward . . . Forward . . ."

Beem responded to the urging. And then stopped once more.

"Forward!"

Beem rushed ahead, like the last time. The quail flew up with a strong beating of wings. And Beem lunged to chase the bird, but—a tug on the leash pulled him back.

"Back!" shouted his master. "No, no!"

Beem tumbled and fell. He couldn't understand why he was

13

being treated like that. And he pulled at the leash in the direction of the bird.

"Lie down!"

Beem lay down.

And this was repeated, with a new quail. But this time Beem felt the tug of the leash earlier and lay down when ordered, trembling with excitement, passion, and at the same time sadness and despair; it was written all over him from his nose to his tail. It hurt so much! Not only the cruel, repulsive leash, but the prickles inside the collar.

"There, there, Beem. Nothing can be done—that's the way it has to be." Ivan Ivanovich stroked Beem to soothe him.

And that was the day he started becoming a real gun dog. That day Beem learned that he, and only he, could tell where there was a bird, and that his master was helpless because the nose he had was only for show. Beem's real work began, based on three words: "no," "back," and "good."

And then—ah!—then came the gun. A shot. The quail plummeted.

And there was no need to chase it, it turned out; he only had to find it, lift its wing, and lie down. His friend did the rest. They were evenly matched: the master had no sense of smell; the dog had no gun.

Thus, warm friendship and loyalty turned into happiness, because each understood the other and neither demanded more from the other than he could give. And this is the very salt of friendship.

By the age of two, Beem had become an excellent hunting dog, trusting and honest. He had a vocabulary of some hundred words relating to hunting and home: if Ivan Ivanovich said "fetch," he did; if he said "fetch my slippers," he did; "bring your bowl," he brought it; "on the chair," and he sat on the chair. But that was nothing. He could tell a lot from his master's

14

eyes. If his master looked kindly at a man, then he was an acquaintance immediately as far as Beem was concerned. If he gave him a hostile look, then Beem might even growl at him. He could even catch flattery (gentle flattery) in a stranger's voice. But Beem never, ever bit anyone—even if the person stepped on his tail. He was happy to warn his master that someone was approaching their campfire at night, but biting—under no circumstances. That was what an intelligent breed meant.

Beem even figured out for himself that he should scratch at the door when he wanted it opened. There were times when Ivan Ivanovich was sick and, instead of taking Beem for a walk, let him out on his own. Beem would run around a bit, take care of his business, and hurry home. He would scratch at the door, whine a little, and the door would open. His master, padding heavily in the entryway, would greet him, pet him, and then get back into bed. This would happen on the days when Ivan Ivanovich, an elderly man, wasn't feeling well (he was sick more and more often, a fact Beem noticed only too well). Beem had mastered it: Scratch at the door and it will certainly be opened; that's what doors are for, to let in anyone who wants to come in. Just ask and they'll let you in. From a dog's point of view, this was a certainty.

Beem didn't know, didn't know and couldn't have known, that there are doors that never open no matter how much you scratch at them.

One thing must be said: Beem, a dog with an excellent sense of smell, still remained a doubtful case—he was not given a certificate of pedigree. Ivan Ivanovich showed him twice, and he was removed from the ring without a rating. That meant he was an outcast from his breed.

Yet Beem was no hereditary incongruity, he was a marvelous, real dog. He began working birds at eight months—superbly! One would like to believe that he had a good future unfolding before him.

15

2

SPRING FOREST

For the second season—that is, in Beem's third year—Ivan Ivanovich introduced him to the forest. This was fascinating for both man and dog.

In the meadows and fields, everything is clear—open spaces, grass, ripening grain, you can always see your master, you can sniff around in a wide-ranging search, seek, find, point, and wait for the command. Marvelous! But here in the forest it's another matter altogether.

It was early spring.

When they got there the first time, the sun was just setting and it was already dusk among the trees, even though there were no leaves yet. Everything below was painted in somber colors: the tree trunks, last year's dark-brown leaves, the brownish-gray stalks of grass, and even the fruits of the nettle, deep ruby in the fall, were like coffee beans now, after the long winter.

The branches swayed and rustled in the breeze, naked and sparse; they seemed to be touching one another with their tips and cuddling the full length of their twigs: Are you still alive? The crowns of the trees swayed lightly—the trees seemed alive even without their leaves. Everything about the forest rustled mysteriously and was deeply scented: the trees, and the leaves underfoot, and the soft, spring-smelling soil, and Ivan Ivanovich's steps, careful and quiet. His shoes rustled, too, and his tracks smelled much stronger than they did in the fields. Something unfamiliar and mysterious hid behind every tree. That's why Beem never went more than twenty paces from Ivan Ivanovich; he would run off, to the left or right, and scurry back, look up into his face, and ask, "Why are we here?"

"You don't know what's going on, do you?" Ivan Ivanovich asked. "You'll understand, Beem, you will. Wait a bit."

And so they walked on, watching over each other.

And then they stopped in a wide meadow at the intersection of two clearings; roads went off in four directions. Ivan Ivanovich stood behind a hazel tree, facing the sunset, and looked up. Beem looked over in that direction, too, trying with all his might to figure out what they were looking for.

It was light up there, but here below it was getting darker and darker. Someone moved through the forest and stopped. Then moved again and grew still. Beem brushed up against Ivan Ivanovich's leg—asking, "What's that? Who is it? Maybe we should go see?"

"A hare," his master said softly. "Everything's all right, Beem. All right. A hare. Let him run around."

Well, if it's "all right," then it's all right. "Hare" he understood, too; many a time when Beem came across the scent, he was told the word. And once he saw a hare, tried to catch it, but was reprimanded and punished for it. No, no!

So, a hare rustled nearby. And then what?

Suddenly, above them, someone, unseen and unknown, cried out, "Hor-hor! Hor-hor! Hor-hor!" Beem heard it first and shuddered. His master did, too. Both looked up. Unexpectedly, against the purple sunset, a bird appeared in the distance. It was flying straight at them, calling out like an animal, not a bird, flying and calling. But it was a bird. It seemed big, and its wings were noiseless (not like a quail, a partridge, or a duck). In other words, something unknown was flying up above.

17

Ivan Ivanovich raised his gun. Beem, as though ordered to, lay down, never taking his eyes from the bird. In the forest the shot was so loud and sharp, Beem had never heard it like that. It resounded through the forest and died away, far, far away.

The bird fell into the brush, but the friends found it quickly. Ivan Ivanovich put it in front of Beem and said, "Get acquainted, brother; this is a woodcock." And he repeated it. "Woodcock."

Beem sniffed it, touched its long beak, then sat down, pawing the ground with his front paws in excitement and amazement. Of course, what he was saying to himself was: "I've never seen a nose like that before. Now that's some nose!"

The forest still made noises, but more and more quietly. And then it hushed, all at once somehow, as though some invisible wing moved strongly over the trees one last time: Enough rustling. The branches became immobile, and the trees seemed to be falling asleep, shuddering now and again in the semidarkness.

Three other woodcocks flew past, but Ivan Ivanovich did not shoot. They couldn't see the last one in the dark; they only heard its call. But Beem was still surprised: Why didn't his friend at least shoot at those they could see? It made Beem anxious. Ivan Ivanovich was simply staring up into the sky, or looking down, listening to the silence. They both were silent.

That's a time when words are unnecessary—for man and certainly for dog!

Only later, as they were leaving, Ivan Ivanovich said, "It's good, Beem! Life is starting anew. It's spring."

Beem could tell from the sound of his voice that his friend felt good. And he nuzzled Ivan Ivanovich's knee, wagging his tail, as if to say: Of course it's good, that goes without saying!

The second time, they came late in the morning, but without the gun.

The aromatic burgeoning buds of the birches, the mighty

18

scents of the roots, the fine streams coming from the shoots of grass breaking through the soil—it was all amazingly new and wonderful. The sun penetrated everything in the forest except the pines, and even there, golden rays cut through the dense needles. And it was quiet. Most important—it was quiet. How good the springtime-morning quiet in the forest!

This time, Beem was braver; everything could be seen clearly (not like the other time at twilight). And he raced around the forest as much as he wanted—without losing sight of his master, however. It was all marvelous.

Finally Beem stumbled onto the thread of a woodcock scent. And he stretched out. And threw a classic point. Ivan Ivanovich sent him "forward," but he had nothing with which to shoot. And then he ordered him to lie still, the way you're supposed to when the bird flies up. It was absolutely confusing; could his master see it or not? Beem squinted sideways at him until he was satisfied that Ivan Ivanovich did see it.

They repeated the procedure with the next woodcock. Beem was beginning to express something like resentment: tense gaze, sidelong trot, even attempts at disobedience—in a word, his resentment was growing and seeking an outlet. And that's why Beem chased the third woodcock when it flew up, just like an ordinary mutt. But you can't chase a woodcock far; it flashes in the branches, and it's gone. Beem came back unsatisfied, and on top of that he was punished. Well, he lay down away off and sighed deeply (dogs are very good at doing that).

He could have taken all that if a second insult hadn't been added. Beem discovered a new flaw in his master—a perverted sense of smell. He had a bad nose anyway, and then—

This is what happened.

Ivan Ivanovich stopped and looked all around and sniffed (hah!). Then he walked over to a tree, sat down, and gently, with one finger, caressed a flower, a tiny one (for Ivan Ivanovich, it had almost no odor, but for Beem it stank to the point of pain).

19

And what did he see in that flower, anyway? But his master sat there and smiled. Beem, of course, pretended to be somewhat pleased with it, too, but that was strictly out of politeness. Actually, he was quite surprised.

"Look, Beem, just take a look at that!" Ivan Ivanovich exclaimed and pressed the dog's nose to the flower.

Beem couldn't bear that. He turned away. Then he quickly walked off and lay in a clearing, his whole manner saying, "Well, go ahead and smell your stupid flower!" Their differences needed immediate clarification and making up, but his master was laughing a happy laugh right in Beem's face. And that hurt. "Go ahead and laugh!"

And Ivan Ivanovich went back to his flower.

"Hello, first one!"

Beem understood only one thing: the hello was not for him.

Jealousy crept into the dog's heart. That's what happened. And although things seemed back to normal at home, Beem was unhappy with the day: there was game, and they didn't shoot; he chased after a bird himself and got punished; and then there was that flower. No, even a dog can have a dog's life, for he lives on the basis of three little words: "no" "back," and "good."

But they didn't know, neither Beem nor Ivan Ivanovich, that one day that morning, if they thought back on it, would seem enormously happy.

From His Master's Notes

In the forest exhausted by winter, when the awakened buds haven't yet opened, when the sorrowful stumps of winter felling haven't begun new growth but have started weeping, when the dead brown leaves lie flat, when the naked branches haven't yet begun to rustle but merely touch one another—I suddenly smelled a crocus! It was barely noticeable, but it was the smell of awakening life, and that's why it brings tremulous joy. I looked around, and it turned out to be nearby. The flower stood on the ground, a tiny drop of the blue sky, a simple and ingenuous herald of happiness for him who is fated to have it. But it is an ornament in the life of everyone—lucky and unlucky.

And that's the way it is among us humans; there are modest people with pure hearts, "unobtrusive" and "small," but with enormous souls. And they're the ones who decorate life, representing all that's best—kindness, simplicity, trust. And so the crocus seems like a drop of sky on earth.

And a few days later (yesterday), Beem and I were back at the same spot. The sky had sprinkled the forest with thousands of blue drops. I sought the very first one, the bravest one: Where are you? That must be it. Is it? I don't know. There are so many that you can't find the one—it's lost among the ones that followed, blended in with them. And it was so small yet heroic, so quiet yet steadfast, that it seemed to scare off the last frosts, making them give up and throw out the white flag of hoarfrost on the edge of the forest in the early dawn. Life goes on.

Beem can't understand any of this. He was even hurt by it the first time; he was jealous. However, when there was a mass of flowers, he no longer paid any attention to them. And he was bad at training; he's upset that there's no gun. He and I are on different levels of development, but very, very close. Nature creates according to a stable principle: the need of one for the other. From the simplest forms to the highest, this law applies. How could I have stood the horrible loneliness without Beem?

How I needed *her! She* loved crocuses, too. The past is like a dream.

Isn't the present a dream? Isn't yesterday's spring forest with the blue ground a dream? Well, sky-blue dreams are a miraculous medicine, even if the effect is temporary. Of course, it's only temporary. If writers preached only blue dreams, leaving gray behind, men would stop worrying about the future, accepting the present as a constant. Our sense of doom about time lies in the fact that the present must become the past. Man hasn't the power to order the sun to stop. Time cannot be stopped, held back, or placated. Time and movement are all. And he who seeks only the stability of sky-blue peace is living in the past, whether he is young or old. Blue has its own sound, the sound of peace, oblivion, but it is only temporary, a respite; and those moments should never be missed.

If I were a writer, I would certainly write: "O restless Man! Glory to you unto the ages, thinking and suffering for the future! If you want to rest your soul, go into the forest in early spring to see the crocuses, and you will see the marvelous dream of reality. Go quickly; in a few days the crocuses may be gone, and you won't be able to capture the magic of that vision given us by nature. Go, rest. Crocuses bring luck, the folk saying goes."

Beem is fast asleep. And he's dreaming; his legs are jerking —he's running in his sleep. He couldn't care less about crocuses; light blue he sees as gray (that's the way dogs see). Nature has created a way of darkening reality. Try to convince him to see things from a human point of view? You could break your head and he'd still see things his way. A totally independent hound.

3

BEEM'S FIRST FOE

The summer passed, a happy one for Beem, filled with friendship. Expeditions into fields and swamps (without a gun), sunny days, swimming, quiet evenings on the riverbank—what more could any dog want? Nothing, surely.

During their training sessions they ran into hunters. They made friends with them immediately, because each man was accompanied by a dog. Even before the men got together, both dogs ran toward each other and communicated briefly in the language of movements and looks.

"What are you, male or female?" Beem asked, sniffing the appropriate parts (*pro forma*, naturally).

"You can see for yourself; why do you ask?" she replied.

"How's life?" Beem asked merrily.

"We're working!" she answered with a squeal, coquettishly jumping up from the ground.

Then they raced back to their owners and told them about their meeting. And when the hunters sat down to talk in the shade of a tree or bush, the dogs played until their tongues couldn't fit in their mouths. Then they, too, lay down, near their masters, and listened to the quiet conversation.

People other than hunters didn't interest Beem; they were just people, that's all. They were nice. But they weren't hunters!

But dogs—there were all different kinds of dogs.

Once in a meadow he met a shaggy little dog, half his size. She was all black. They greeted each other with restraint and no flirtation. There could be no thought of flirting, since his new acquaintance answered the usual set of questions with a lazy wag of her tail, like this: "I'm hungry."

She had mouse on her breath. And Beem inquired in surprise, sniffing her lips, "You ate a mouse?"

"I ate a mouse," she replied. "I'm hungry." And she started chewing on the white, sinewy root of a reed.

Beem wanted to taste it, but she protested with the same old: "I'm hungry."

Beem sat and waited for her to finish it up and asked her to join him. She accepted with a murmur, jogging behind him, disheveled but clean (apparently she enjoyed swimming, as do most dogs, which is why there are no dirty dogs in summer— even the strays are clean). Beem brought her over to his master, who had been observing their meeting from a distance. But Shaggy didn't trust the strange man right away, and sat a few feet off, even though Beem ran back and forth between them, calling her, convincing her. Ivan Ivanovich took off his backpack, took out some sausage, cut off a small piece, and tossed it to Shaggy, saying, "Come here, Shaggy, come here."

The piece fell some three yards away from her. Moving carefully, she reached the meat, ate it, and sat down on the spot. The next piece brought her closer. And then she sat at the man's feet; she even allowed him to pet her, but warily. Beem and Ivan Ivanovich gave her the whole ring of sausage; the master threw the pieces, and Beem did not interfere with Shaggy's meal. It was the usual thing: throw a piece—she'll come closer; another piece—closer still; and with the third and fourth pieces she'll be at your feet and serve with loyalty and truth. That's what Ivan Ivanovich thought. He felt Shaggy all over, ruffled her head, and said, "Your nose is cold. That means you're healthy. Good." And he gave the command to both of them: "Go run!"

24

Shaggy didn't know those words, but when she saw Beem racing through the grass she understood: I'm supposed to run. And of course they began a romp that made Beem forget why he was there. Ivan Ivanovich didn't stop them and just walked along whistling.

Shaggy accompanied them readily as far as the city, but at the outskirts she suddenly sat down at the side of the road—and wouldn't budge. They called; they cajoled; she wouldn't move. And so she remained there, watching them disappear from view. Ivan Ivanovich was wrong—it's not every dog that can be bought with food.

Beem didn't know and couldn't have known that Shaggy had her own masters, that they had lived in a little house, that their block had been razed, and that Shaggy's owners had been given an apartment with all the conveniences on the fifth floor.

In other words, Shaggy had been abandoned. But she had managed to find the new house, and her owners' door; and they beat her and chased her away. And so she lived on her own. She went into the city only at night, like most homeless dogs. Ivan Ivanovich had guessed her story, but it was impossible to explain it to Beem. Beem simply didn't want to leave her; he kept looking back, stopping and gazing up at Ivan Ivanovich. But his master just went on walking.

If he had known how bitter fate would bring Beem and Shaggy together, if he knew when and where they would meet, he wouldn't have walked along so calmly. But man does not know the future, either.

The third summer passed. It was a good summer for Beem and not a bad one for Ivan Ivanovich. One night he shut the window and said, "A frost, Beem, the first frost."

Beem did not understand. He got up and nuzzled Ivan Ivanovich's knee in the dark, which was his way of saying, "I don't understand."

25

Ivan Ivanovich knew dog language well—the language of gestures and eyes. He turned on the light and asked, "You don't understand, you silly?" Then he explained, "We go after woodcock tomorrow. Woodcock!"

Oh, that was a word Beem knew well! He jumped up and licked his friend on the chin.

"Tomorrow we hunt, Beem!"

Hurrah! Beem began spinning like a top, chasing his own tail, squealed, and sat down, the fine hair on his forelegs trembling, staring at Ivan Ivanovich. Beem knew the bewitching word "hunt" as the key to happiness.

But his master ordered, "And for now—sleep." He put out the light and went to bed.

Beem spent the rest of the night by his friend's bed. How could he sleep! Both of them dozed on and off, waking often in anticipation of dawn.

In the morning they packed the backpack, oiled the guns, had a light breakfast (you can't fill up too much when you hunt), checked the ammunition, moving the shells from chamber to chamber. There was a lot of work to do in that brief hour of preparation: the man would go into the kitchen, so would Beem; the man would go into the storeroom, so would Beem; the man would take a can of food out of the pack (it didn't fit comfortably); the man would check the shells, and Beem watched (so that the man made no mistake); and then he had to stick his nose into the gun carrier several times (is it in there for sure?); and then, of course, it was always at important times like this that you got an itch behind your ear, and you had to lift your leg and scratch—phooey, just when you were at your busiest.

Well, they were finally ready. Beem was ecstatic. And why not? His master, already wearing his hunting jacket, tossed his game bag over his shoulder, and took his gun.

"To the hunt, Beem, to the hunt!" his eyes said, and Beem was entranced. He was even whining slightly in his overwhelming feeling of gratitude and love for his only friend in the entire world.

A man walked in just then. Beem knew him—he had seen him around in the courtyard—but he considered him of little interest and not worthy of any particular attention. Short-legged, fat, and broad-faced, the man said in a hoarse bass voice, "Greetings, I say!" And he sat down, wiping his face with a handkerchief. "So—going hunting, I see?"

"Hunting," Ivan Ivanovich grumbled, "for woodcock. Why don't you join us—you'll be our guest."

"So—hunting, eh? I say, you'll have to put it off."

Beem looked back and forth at his master and the Visitor, surprised and attentive.

Ivan Ivanovich said grumpily, "I don't understand what you mean. Explain."

And Beem, our gentle Beem, growled and then gave a quick bark. He had never done such a thing in his entire life—bark in their own home, and at a guest, at that. The Visitor wasn't frightened; he seemed quite unimpressed.

"Go to your place!" Ivan Ivanovich ordered angrily.

Beem obeyed; he lay down on his bed, head on his paws, and kept looking at the stranger.

"Well, well! I see, he listens. So. So, he barks at the tenants on the stairs the way he does at foxes?"

"Never. Never and at no one. This is the first time. My word of honor!" Ivan Ivanovich was upset and angry. "By the way, he has nothing to do with foxes."

"So," the Visitor said once more. "Let's get down to business."

Ivan Ivanovich took off his jacket and cap. "I'm listening."

"So, you have a dog," the Visitor said. "And I have," he said, "a complaint about it." He took a piece of paper from his pocket. "Here." He gave the paper to Beem's owner.

Ivan Ivanovich was visibly upset by what he read. Beem, seeing this, got up from his bed without permission and sat at his master's feet, in order to defend him, but he no longer looked at the Visitor, even though he was alert and ready.

"This is nonsense," Ivan Ivanovich said more calmly. "Sheer nonsense. Beem is a gentle dog. He's never bitten anyone and never will; he wouldn't hurt anyone. He's an intelligent dog."

"Ho-ho-ho!" The Visitor's belly shook with laughter. And then he sneezed. "Oh, you flunky, you!" he said to Beem without any anger.

Beem turned away even more, but he knew that they were talking about him. And he sighed.

"Is this how you take care of complaints?" Ivan Ivanovich asked, now completely calm and smiling. "The subject of the complaint shouldn't be reading it. I would have taken you at your word."

Beem noticed laughter in the Visitor's eyes. He said, "First of all, this is the procedure. Secondly, the complaint isn't against you, it's against the dog. And we won't let the dog read it." He laughed.

The master laughed, too, a little. Beem didn't even smile; he knew they were talking about him, but he couldn't understand what they were saying—that Visitor was very confusing. He pointed in Beem's direction and said, "The dog must leave." And he waved in the direction of the door.

Beem knew that they wanted him to leave. But he didn't budge an inch from his master's side.

"Why don't you call in the complainant—we'll talk, maybe work things out," Ivan Ivanovich asked.

In response, the Visitor got up and soon came back with a woman. "Here, I brought her."

Beem knew her, too. She was short, squealy, and fat, and she spent the entire day sitting on the bench in the yard with the other idle women in the building. Once Beem even

28

licked her hand (not from overflowing feelings for her personally, but for humanity in general), and she squealed and started shouting all over the yard, addressing herself to the open windows. He didn't know what she was shouting, but Beem got scared, ran out of there, and scratched at his door to get in. That was his only crime against the Woman. And here she was. Poor Beem! He cringed behind his owner's legs, and, after being petted, tucked in his tail and went to his bed, staring up at her meekly. He couldn't understand anything of what she said, and she gabbed on and on, and kept showing them her hand. And that gesture and her angry looks explained it to Beem; this all happened because he licked the wrong person. Beem was young—too young—and he didn't think straight yet. Perhaps he was thinking, "I'm guilty, I admit it; but what can I do now?" At least, there was something like that in his eyes.

Only Beem didn't know he was being falsely accused.

"He wanted to bite me! Bite me! He almost bit me!"

Ivan Ivanovich, interrupting her chatter, turned to Beem: "Beem! Bring me my slippers!"

Beem did so readily and lay down in front of his master.

He took off his hunting boots and put on the slippers. "Now take my boots away."

Beem did that too; he took one and then the other to the closet.

The woman shut up, her eyes bugging. The Visitor applauded Beem: "Fine fellow! Look at that; he knows how to do that." And he gave the woman an unfriendly look. "Can he do anything else?"

"Sit down, sit down," Ivan Ivanovich invited the woman.

She sat down, tucking her hands under her apron. His master offered Beem a chair and ordered him to sit on it.

Beem didn't need to be told twice. Now they were all sitting on chairs. The woman bit her lip. The Visitor, swinging his leg

29

in satisfaction, was muttering to himself, "It's turning out fine, just fine."

The master slyly squinted in Beem's direction and said, "Shake hands." And he extended his hand.

They shook hands.

"Now, silly, shake with our Visitor." And he pointed at him. The man offered his hand. "Hello, fellow. I say, hello."

Beem did it elegantly, just the way one should.

"He won't bite?" the woman asked cautiously.

"Don't be silly!" Ivan Ivanovich said. "Put out your hand and say 'Shake.'"

And she took her hand out from under her apron and extended it to Beem. "Just don't bite," she warned.

Well, it's impossible to describe what happened. Beem made a beeline for his bed, rolled up in a defensive position, his back against the corner, and stared at his master. Ivan Ivanovich went over to him, petted him, took him by the collar, and brought him back.

"Shake hands, shake—"

No, Beem wouldn't shake. He turned away and stared at the floor. It was the first time he had disobeyed. And he grimly went back to the corner, slowly, guiltily, and stubbornly.

Oh! What a scene that caused! The woman went on and on like a broken record.

"You've insulted me!" she shouted at Ivan Ivanovich. "Some lousy, mangy dog spurns me, a Soviet woman!" She pointed at Beem. "Why, I'll—I'll—You just wait!"

"Cut it out!" the Visitor barked at her. "You're crazy. That dog didn't bite you and had no intention of doing it. It's as afraid of you as the Devil is of prayer."

"Don't you shout," she said.

Then the Visitor said unambiguously, "Shut up!" And he turned to Beem's master. "It's the only way with people like that." And then back to the woman. "Boy! 'A Soviet woman,'

30

indeed. Get out of here! If you make trouble one more time, I'll shame you. Get out, I say!" He tore up the complaint in front of her face.

Beem understood the Visitor's last speech very well. The woman left in silence, head raised high and looking at no one, while Beem didn't take his eyes off her and continued looking at the door long after she had left and her footsteps had died down.

"You were quite—rough on her," Ivan Ivanovich said.

"It's the only way, I tell you. She'll have the whole building in an uproar, I know. So, it means I know what I'm talking about. I've had it up to here with these gossips and troublemakers," he said and patted his throat. "She's got nothing to do, so she sits around and plots whom to bite next. You give people like that free rein and the whole house will be infested."

Beem kept watching the expressions, gestures, and tone of voice, and understood that the Visitor and his master were not enemies at all, and probably respected each other. He observed them for a long time, while they chatted about something else. But once he had established the one important fact, the rest didn't interest him very much. He went over to the Visitor and lay down near his feet, as though to say "I'm sorry."

From His Master's Notes

Today, the chairman of the building committee was here to take care of a complaint against the dog. Beem won. Actually, my visitor judged the case with the wisdom of Solomon. A self-made Solomon.

Why did Beem growl at him at the beginning? Aha, I've got it! I didn't shake hands with him and greeted him coldly (I had to put off our hunting trip), and Beem was acting in accordance with his nature: The master's foe is my foe. And I'm the one who

31

should be ashamed here, not Beem. His ability to interpret minute changes in tone, expression, or gesture is amazing! I have to keep that in mind constantly.

Afterward, the chairman and I had an interesting talk. He now uses the informal "you" with me.

"You," he says, "just think. There are a hundred and fifty apartments in my house! And four or five troublemakers can turn this place upside down, so that no one will be able to live peacefully. Everyone knows them, and everyone's afraid of them; yet secretly they support them. Even the toilet bowl gurgles at a bad tenant. I swear! You know my worst enemy? Anyone who doesn't work. People can get by in our society without working, feeding from the common bowl. There's something wrong in that if you ask me. Wrong, I say. You can get away without working! Just think! What do you do, for instance?"

"I write," I said, not knowing whether he was joking or not (people with a sense of humor often say serious things in the guise of a joke).

"Is that work? You sit around and don't do anything, and you still get paid, I'll bet."

"I get paid, but I don't get very much. I'm getting on; I'm living on a pension."

"And before you retired, what did you do?"

"I was a journalist. I worked for the papers. And now I write a bit at home."

"You write?" he asked in a condescending way.

"I write."

"Well, write on, if that's what you do. Of course, you're all right, I can tell, but you see—that's the problem. I'm also retired. I get a hundred rubles, but I still work as the chairman of the building committee; and I work for free, keep that in mind. I'm used to working; I was always in management, and I was never demoted. They tried toward the end and kept sending me to smaller and smaller places. My last job was in a tiny plant. And that's where my pension was awarded me. They didn't give me a special one—there was a loophole. Everyone must work. That's what I think."

"But my work is hard, too," I tried to justify myself.

"Writing, you mean? Nonsense. If you were a young man, I'd straighten you out. But if you're on a pension and all . . . But with the young ones, if they don't work I get them out of the building. Work or ship out, that's what I say."

He really is the scourge of the loafers in our house. I think the main goal of his life is to get rid of all the loafers, wastrels, and parasites, but lecturing everyone without exception is also one of his activities. Convincing him that writing is also work was impossible; he either made sly jokes or merely patronized me (let him write—there are worse loafers to deal with now).

He was kind and dropped his usual joking manner as he left. He patted Beem and said, "So you live on here, I say. But don't get mixed up with that woman." And then to me he said, "Well, go on, write. What can I do if that's what your job is."

We shook hands warmly. Beem walked him to the door, waving his tail and looking up into his eyes. Beem had a new friend: Pavel Titych Rydayev, usually called "Paltitych."

But Beem had also acquired a foe: the woman, the only person he doesn't trust. The dog has met a slanderer.

Our hunting was ruined today. It happens like that sometimes; you expect a good day, and all you get is problems. It happens.

4

THE YELLOW FOREST

A few days later, early in the morning, they left the house together. First they rode the trolley, out on the platform. The conductor turned out to be a friend of Ivan Ivanovich and Beem. Naturally Beem greeted her when she came out to change the switch. She scratched him behind the ear, but Beem didn't lick her hand, he only moved his front paws up and down as he sat and beat out an appropriate greeting with his tail.

Then, outside the city limits, they rode on a bus, which had five or six passengers even at that hour of the morning. As they were getting on, the driver began grumbling about something, repeating the words "dog" and "not allowed." Beem easily understood that the driver didn't want to let them on, and that was bad—he figured it out from the frowns. One of the passengers came to their defense; another backed up the driver. Beem watched the fracas with lively interest. Finally the driver got out of the bus. Ivan Ivanovich gave him a yellow piece of paper at the door and went up the steps with Beem, sat down, and sighed sadly.

Beem had noticed a long time ago that people exchanged these pieces of paper that had no one definite smell. Once, he realized that one of them on the table smelled of blood, and he nuzzled it to get his master's attention, but Ivan Ivanovich didn't bat an eye—no sense of smell!—and just went on with his "no-no." And then he locked up the papers in his desk. Other pieces of paper, while they're clean, smell of bread, sausage—stores in general—but most of them smell of many hands. People love those papers and hide them in their pockets or desks, like Beem's master. Beem didn't really know anything about these matters, but he understood that as soon as his master gave the driver the paper they became friends. And Beem didn't know why his master sighed, which was apparent from his attentive gaze into Ivan Ivanovich's eyes. In general he didn't have the foggiest idea of the magical powers of the papers; he didn't know that one day they would perform a fateful service for him.

They walked from the highway to the forest.

Ivan Ivanovich stopped at the edge of the forest to rest, and Beem checked out the area. He had never seen a forest like this before. Actually, it was the same forest they had visited in the spring and in the summer (just for an outing), but now everything was yellow and crimson; it seemed that everything was burning and glowing with the sun.

The trees were only beginning to shed their garments, and the leaves fell, swaying in the air, silently and smoothly. The air was cool and fresh, and it made Beem happy. The autumnal smell of the forest, so special, inimitable, pure, and strong, allowed Beem to smell his master dozens of yards away. He "received" the scent of a field mouse at a great distance, but he didn't go after it (it was a familiar trifle!); then something live hit him in the nose with enough force to stop him in his tracks. And when he got right up next to it, he barked and barked at the prickly ball.

Ivan Ivanovich got up from a tree stump and went over to see what Beem was doing.

"No, Beem! No, silly. It's called a hedgehog. Back!" And he led Beem away.

Now Ivan Ivanovich sat down again, ordered Beem to sit, too, took off his cap, set it down next to him on the ground, and looked at the leaves. And listened to the stillness of the forest. And of course he smiled! That is the way he always was before the hunt.

Beem listened, too.

A magpie flew down, chattered at them insolently, and flew off. A jay hopped from branch to branch, screamed at them with a cat's howl, and hopped off again. And then came the call of a kinglet: "Sweet, sweet!" What can you do with a little fellow like that! No bigger than a bug, and he keeps calling out: "Sweet, sweet!" Like a welcome.

Everything else was silence.

And now his master stood up, unwrapped his gun, and loaded it. Beem quivered with excitement. Ivan Ivanovich petted him and ruffled his neck, which made Beem even more excited.

"Well, little one—seek!"

Beem was off! He hurried away, skirting the trees, close to the ground, with a springy gait, almost noiselessly. Ivan Ivanovich followed quietly, enjoying his friend's work. Now the forest with all its splendors fell into the background; Beem, exquisite, passionate, light-footed, Beem was important. His master would call him over once in a while so that Beem would calm down a bit. And soon Beem went on steadily, knowing his work. The setter's work is a great art! There he goes in an easy lope, head raised—he doesn't need to keep it down to pick up scents; he can do that up high. And his silky hair lies close on his chiseled neck—that's what makes him so beautiful, the way he holds his head high, with dignity, confidence, and passion.

Those hours were hours of oblivion for Ivan Ivanovich. He would forget the war, the bitterness of his past life, and his loneliness. Even his son Kolya, his child taken away by the ruthless war, seemed to be near him, as if, even in death, Kolya enjoyed his father. He had been a hunter, too! The dead don't disappear from the lives of those who loved them, and they don't age but continue in the hearts of the living just as they were when they departed. That's the way it was with Ivan Ivanovich: the wounds had formed scar tissue in his heart, but they went on hurting. But when one is hunting, any psychic pain is lessened, even if only a tiny bit. Blessed is he who was born a hunter.

And now Beem was slowing down, narrowing his cast; he stopped for a split second and then went on stealthily. There was something catlike in his movements, soft, cautious, fluid. His head was stretched out in line with his body. Every part of his body, including the extended tasseled tail, was concentrated on the stream of the scent. A step—and then only one foot came up. A step—and the next foot also stopped in midair for a fraction of a second and came down silently. Finally the right foreleg, as usual, froze just above the ground.

Gun ready, Ivan Ivanovich came up from behind. Now there were two statues: man and dog.

The forest was silent. The golden leaves of the birches played quietly, bathed in the reflected sunlight. The young oaks were hushed beside the giant oak tree, their father and ancestor. The few remaining silver-gray leaves on the aspen trembled noiselessly. And the dog—one of the best creations of nature—and a patient man stood on the carpet of yellow leaves. Not a single muscle quivered! In moments like this, Beem seemed halfdead, as if in a trance brought on by rapture and passion—a classic setter's point in a yellow forest.

"Forward, boy."

Beem flushed the woodcock.

Bam!

The forest trembled and replied with a grumpy, insulted echo. The birches that had crept up on the oak and aspen groves shuddered in fright. The oaks grunted like giant warriors. The aspen right next to them quickly shed its last leaves.

The woodcock fell like a lump. Beem turned it over and

picked it up, following all the regulations. But his master, caressing Beem and thanking him for his beautiful work, looked at the bird in his hand and said thoughtfully, "Ah, I should have. . . ."

Beem didn't understand and kept peering into his master's face. Ivan Ivanovich went on, "Only for you, Beem, for you, you silly. Otherwise—it wasn't worth it."

And Beem didn't understand. He couldn't. And during the entire hunt, Beem felt that his master was shooting like a blind man. And the dog was very unhappy when his master didn't even take a shot at one of the woodcocks Beem had flushed. But at least he brought down the last one cleanly.

They got home after dark, tired and gentle with each other. Beem, for instance, didn't want to spend the night in his own bed and dragged his blanket over to the floor beside Ivan Ivanovich's bed and lay down on it. His reasoning was that he couldn't be sent back to his "place," since he had brought it with him. Ivan Ivanovich rumpled his ear and his ruff. It seemed their friendship would last forever.

But that night Ivan Ivanovich moaned quietly, got up, swallowed pills, and went back to bed. Beem listened guardedly at first, watching his friend, then got up and licked the hand dangling from the bed.

"Shrapnel—it's the shrapnel, Beem. It's moving around. It's bad, boy," said Ivan Ivanovich, holding his hand over his heart.

Beem knew the word "bad" very well. And he'd heard the word "shrapnel" several times. He didn't understand it, but his intuition told him that it was a troublesome word, a bad word, a horrible one.

But everything turned out all right. In the morning, after their walk, Ivan Ivanovich sat down at his desk as usual, put down a fresh sheet of white paper, and whispered across it with his stick.

From His Master's Notes

Yesterday was a happy day. Everything was just perfect: autumn, the yellow forest, Beem's exquisite work. But still, there's an unpleasant aftertaste. Why?

Beem clearly noticed me sigh in the bus, and he obviously understood my feelings. The dog can't imagine that I gave the bus driver a bribe. A dog doesn't give a darn about that. And me? What's the difference whether I give a ruble for a small "favor," or twenty for a big one, or a thousand for a major one? It's still shameful. Like selling your conscience for trifles. Of course, Beem is much lower than a human being, so he will never even have an inkling of that.

Beem will never understand that those pieces of paper and a man's conscience are often directly connected. But what a fool I'm being! You can't demand more of a dog than it's capable of; you can't turn a dog into a human.

And another thing: I don't like killing game anymore. Must be old age. It was all so beautiful, and then suddenly there was a dead bird. . . . I'm no vegetarian and no hypocrite who talks about the suffering of murdered animals while he gobbles their flesh with pleasure, but I'm making this rule for the rest of my life: only one or two woodcock per outing, no more. It would be even better to kill none, but then Beem will be ruined as a hunting dog, and I'll just have to buy a bird that someone else killed for me. No, spare me that. And whom am I addressing here, anyway? Myself, I guess. After prolonged solitude, a split personality is inevitable to some degree. For centuries, man has been saved from it by the dog.

But why that unpleasant aftertaste from yesterday? And is it only from yesterday? Have I missed something here? So, yesterday in a nutshell: the desire for happiness—and the yellow ruble note; the yellow forest—and the dead bird. What is this?

39

Am I bargaining with my conscience?

Here's the thought that eluded me yesterday: it's not the bargaining, but the pangs of guilt and pain for all those who kill pointlessly while man loses his humanity. My compassion for birds and animals comes from the past, from my memories of the past, and it grows and grows.

I remember.

The Hunting Society authorized killing magpies because they are pests, a ruling allegedly based on the observations of biologists. And hunters killed magpies without a second thought. And wolves. They were almost completely destroyed. A bounty of thirty rubles (in old money) was paid for a wolf, and anyone bringing the Society the feet of a magpie or kite got either five kopecks or fifty kopecks, I don't remember.

But suddenly a new regulation was issued to the effect that kites and magpies are useful birds and not predators; killing them was forbidden. The license to kill them was replaced by a ban on killing them.

There is only one bird now that is subject to unrestricted killing and isn't protected by law, and that's the gray crow. It supposedly destroys other birds' nests (which is something the magpie used to be accused of). But no one is held responsible for the pesticide poisoning of the birds of the steppe and forest. Saving the forests and fields from pests, we are killing the birds, and in killing them, we destroy—the forests. How could that be the fault of the gray crow, the eternal garbage collector and companion of our society?

Blame it all on the gray crow!—that's the fundamental, sure-fire justification used by the guilty.

Did I raise my voice against experiments with death in my day? No. And that's on my conscience now. How pale and weak my voice would sound now if I were to say belatedly: Save the gray crow—an excellent garbage collector in areas of human habitation—save it from extinction because it helps clean up after us just as the satirist cleans the spiritual dirt from our society. Save the gray crow for that reason alone; let it swipe a few birds' eggs. After all, it *is* the gray crow, and its function is to teach birds to build safe nests. Save this brazen mocker who is daring and obnoxious and naive enough to call from a tree top right into a man's face, "Ca-aw!" (Which means, "Get out of here, you jerk!") And as soon as you do, it will fly down and with a jeering croak gobble up a piece of meat so rotten that no dog would ever touch it. Save the gray crow—the satirist of the bird world! Don't be afraid of it. See how the tiny swallows give it friendly pecks to chase it from places that are clean without it, and watch it fly off, croaking spitefully, to a spot that smells rotten. Save the gray crow!

Really, that would have been a weak and unconvincing plea! So let it stay here in my notebook on Beem. I'll write "Beem" on the cover right now. This book will be only for me. After all, I began the notes in the hope of saving Beem's honor, besmirched at his birth, but they're expanding and now include everything that has to do with Beem and with me, too. No one, obviously, is going to publish them. Anyway, who'd be interested in reading "about a dog, about myself"? No one. I'd like to use Koltsov's words:

> I don't write for instant fame:
> But for amusement, entertainment,
> For my friends, sincere and dear,
> For the memory of days past.

And Beem is napping in the daytime—he did so much work, my little friend, and breathed so much of the yellow forest scents.

Ah, the yellow forest! There's a chunk of happiness for you; there's a place for meditation. A man becomes purer in a sunny autumn forest.

41

5

BEATING THE WOODS AT WOLF RAVINE

One autumn day, a man smelling of guns and dogs came to see Ivan Ivanovich. Even though he wasn't carrying any hunting gear and was dressed the way dull people dressed, Beem sensed the fine scent of the woods on him, and the traces of gun on his hands, and the aromatic essence of autumn leaves on his shoes. Naturally Beem reported on all of this, sniffing the Visitor and looking up at his master and energetically wagging his tail. He was seeing the man for the first time but accepted him as a comrade without doubt or hesitation.

The Visitor knew dog language, and so he spoke to Beem gently: "You recognize the hunter in me. Good boy, good." He patted him on the head and said confidently and clearly, "Sit!"

Beem obeyed and sat down, working his paws constantly. And he listened, his eyes fixed on the men.

The Visitor and his master shook hands, their kindly eyes meeting.

"Wonderful!" said Beem, squealing.

"A smart dog," said the Visitor, glancing over at Beem.

"Beem is very good. You couldn't ask for better," Ivan Ivanovich replied.

So that was their little three-way conversation. And then the visiting hunter took a paper from his pocket, spread it out, and started pointing to things on it: "Here—here, in the deepest part of Wolf Ravine, I tried howling. I got five replies—three new ones and two regulars. I saw one. Some wolf, let me tell you!"

Beem knew his master's use of "here-here!" when they hunted. He perked up. But when he heard the word "wolf" he opened his eyes wide; that was the terrible smell of the forest dog that had scared Beem once, the smell his master had explained to him, showing him the tracks: "Wolf! That's a wolf, Beem!" And the Visitor sounded scared when he said the word.

The Visitor left, having said good-bye to Beem, too.

Ivan Ivanovich started packing his cartridges with heavy lead pellets, sprinkling them with potato flour.

Beem slept restlessly that night.

And long before daylight they went outside with the gun and stood on the corner. Soon a truck pulled up, filled with hunters. They were sitting on benches in the covered truck-bed, quietly and solemnly. Ivan Ivanovich helped Beem up first and then got in.

Yesterday's Visitor said, "Oh, no! Why are you taking Beem?"

"There shouldn't be any dogs on a roundup. Take him back!" someone else said. "He'll start making a racket and ruin the roundup."

"Beem won't; he's no hound," Ivan Ivanovich said defensively.

He was opposed by several loud voices at once, but it ended up with yesterday's Visitor saying, "All right. I'll put you and Beem in the rear, Ivan Ivanovich. There's a spot down the streambed where wolves have sometimes broken through the flag line."

Beem had guessed they didn't want to take him and he, too, had tried to talk his neighbors into accepting him, but in the dark no one could tell. Then the truck took off.

The sun was rising by the time they parked by the ranger's station. They all got out quietly and without a word, and so did Beem. Then they went single file along the edge of the forest. No one smoked, no one coughed, no one even kicked his own foot clumsily; they all knew where they were going, why, who, and what. Only Beem didn't know, but he shadowed his master. As they walked, his master touched Beem's ear: Good, Beem, good.

Their leader, walking ahead of them, was yesterday's Visitor. He raised his hand and they all stopped. Three men from the front of the line went into the forest quietly, like cats, and soon returned. Now the leader raised his cap and waved it forward. Half the hunters followed him on this signal, Ivan Ivanovich and Beem behind the rest. Beem was last; no one could move more quietly than he, but his master kept him on a leash, anyway.

On the Leader's wordless command, the first hunter stopped at a bush and froze there. Soon the second halted by an oak stand, and then the third, and, one after the other, the rest. Only Ivan Ivanovich and Beem were left with the Leader. They moved even more carefully than before. Now Beem saw that there was a cord strung along their path, and pieces of fabric that looked like fire hung motionless from it. Finally the Leader left them and went back.

Beem's sensitive ears heard the man's steps long after he left, heard him leading the other hunters to their posts, so far away that even Beem finally couldn't hear.

And silence descended. The tense, anxious silence of the forest. Beem felt it in the way his master stood still, the way his knee was shaking, the way he silently loaded his gun and tensed once more.

They were stationed under cover of a hazel bush on the edge of the stream bed, overgrown with thick thorns. They were surrounded by the mighty oak forest, now silent and stern.

Every tree was a giant warrior. And between the trees the thick underbrush stressed the unique power of the eternal forest.

Beem was all concentrated attention; he sat immobile, catching scents in the air, but he didn't find anything unusual yet, as there was no wind. And that made Beem restless. When there was the slightest breeze, Beem could always tell what was out there, he could read currents of air as though they were lines in a book; but without wind, and in a forest like this—just try to be calm, especially when the kind friend standing next to you is all keyed-up.

And suddenly it began.

The signal shot tore the stillness apart, and the echo careened back and forth in the distance. And then, as if in tune with the forest's clamor, came the Leader's voice: "It's on! Ha-loooo!"

Ivan Ivanovich leaned over to Beem's ear and whispered, barely audibly, "Stay!"

Beem lay down. And he trembled.

"Hal-loooo-oooo!" the beaters roared out there.

The silence had disintegrated into wild, strange, and piercing voices. Sticks were beating against trees, the rattle sounded like a hundred magpies facing their deaths. The chain of beaters was approaching with cries and hullabaloo, firing their guns.

And then—Beem smelled a scent familiar from his youth: wolf! He pressed close to his master's leg and rose up on his feet a bit—just a tiny bit!—and extended his tail. Ivan Ivanovich understood it all.

They both saw it: a wolf was running along the flag line, out of range. He was loping along, head lowered, tail hanging heavily. And then the animal disappeared. Immediately, almost simultaneously, there was a shot from the chain, and then another one.

The forest roared. The forest was excited and angry.

There was another shot. From a nearby station. And the cries were coming closer and closer.

The wolf, a huge old one, appeared unexpectedly. He had come up the stream bed, hidden by the thornbushes, and, seeing the flags, he stopped abruptly, as if stumbling on something. But here, over the bed, the flags were hung higher than on the rest of the line, three times the height of the wolf. And the beaters' noise was coming up behind him. The wolf passed under the flags indecisively and almost indifferently, and ended up fifteen yards from Ivan Ivanovich and Beem. As he covered the distance, the man and the dog had time to see that he was wounded: a bloodstain was spreading on his side, and his mouth was flecked with reddish foam.

Ivan Ivanovich fired.

The wolf jumped up on all four legs, and then turned his whole body sharply, without moving his neck, toward the shot and—stood his ground. The broad, powerful forehead, the bloodshot eyes, bared teeth, and reddish foam—and still he wasn't pathetic. He was beautiful, that free wild beast. Oh, no, he was no coward, he did not want to fall even now, the proud beast, but—he collapsed on his back, slowly bicycling his legs. Then he was still, resigned, calm.

Beem couldn't stand it. He jumped up and threw a point. But what a point it was! His fur was bristling, standing straight up on his ruff, and his tail was between his legs. It was an angry and cowardly, ugly point at his brother, the proud king of dogs, now dead and harmless, but still terrifying for his spirit and his blood. Beem hated his brother. Beem trusted men, and the wolf did not. Beem feared his brother, and the wolf did not fear him even when he was mortally wounded.

The cries were right near them now. There was one more shot. And then a doublet. Apparently an experienced wolf was moving close to the chain and had perhaps broken through at the last moment, when the men were no longer alert and were getting close to one another.

Finally the Leader came out of the underbrush and spoke to

Ivan Ivanovich, with a look at Beem: "Well, well! You don't even look like a dog: a real ferocious beast. Two got away, though. One was wounded."

Ivan Ivanovich petted Beem, stroked him, but Beem, even after his fur had settled smoothly on his back, still ran around in circles, panting, tongue out, shunning the men. When the hunters went over to the wolf, Beem did not follow. Instead, breaking all the rules, he went off dragging his leash and lay down some thirty yards from them, resting his head on the yellow leaves and trembling feverishly. Ivan Ivanovich came closer and saw that the whites of Beem's eyes were bright red. A beast!

"Ah, little Beem. You feel sad? Of course you do. You must. That's the way it has to be, boy."

"Ivan Ivanovich, remember that you can ruin a gun dog with a wolf," the Leader said. "He'll be afraid of the woods. The dog is a slave; the wolf is a free spirit."

"I know, but Beem's already four—a grown dog won't be scared by the woods. On the other hand, he won't leave my side in a forest where there are wolves; he'll come on the scent and say 'wolves!' "

"That's true; wolves will eat a gun dog like a spring chicken. But they won't get the chance with this one; he'll never leave your side once he smells a wolf."

"That's right. You shouldn't scare them with wolves until they're at least a year old. But as for him, what can you do? He has to suffer through this."

Ivan Ivanovich led Beem away, and the Leader stayed with the wolf, waiting for the beaters.

When all the hunters gathered at the ranger's, drinking and talking, excited and pleased, Beem curled up by the fence, aloof and alone, grim, red-eyed, stunned, and infected by the spirit of the wolf. Ah, if only Beem had known that fate would bring him to this very forest again!

47

The ranger came over to him, crouched, and stroked his back. "You're a good dog; yes, you are. A smart dog. You didn't bark once during the whole roundup."

They all loved dogs here.

But when the hunters got in the truck and Ivan Ivanovich put Beem in, the dog jumped out like a scared cat, whimpering and bristling; he did not want to be in there with three dead wolves.

"Aha!" said the Leader. "This one will never get in trouble now."

A burly hunter grudgingly got out of the cab and got in the back so that Ivan Ivanovich and Beem could ride up front.

There weren't too many expeditions for woodcock after that, and Beem worked well, as usual. But he had only to sniff a wolf trail to stop the hunt; he would press against his master's leg and refuse to budge. That was his way of conveying "wolf." And that was good. He loved Ivan Ivanovich even more after the roundup, and believed in his power. Beem believed in man's goodness. It's a great blessing to believe. And to love. A dog without faith is no dog at all, but a free wolf or (even worse) a stray hound. Those are the two choices for any dog that has stopped believing in its master and has left him or been thrown out. Woe to the dog that loses its beloved human friend, for it will seek him and wait for him. It will be unable to become a lone wolf or an ordinary stray, but will remain the same dog it was, faithful and loyal to its missing friend, lonely to the end of its days.

I won't tell you the many true stories about dogs who displayed such fidelity for years—until they died. I will only tell you about Beem with one black ear.

6

FAREWELL TO A FRIEND

One day after a hunting trip, Ivan Ivanovich came home, fed Beem, and went to bed without eating or putting out the light. Beem had worked very hard that day, and so he fell asleep quickly and didn't hear anything. But in the next few days he began noticing that his master was lying down a good deal during the day, that he was bothered by something, and that he gasped with pain from time to time. For more than a week, Beem went out on his own, for brief walks, just to relieve himself. Then Ivan Ivanovich began staying in bed, barely able to get to the door to let Beem in or out. Once he groaned very painfully as he lay in bed. Beem sat by the bed, carefully searching his friend's face, and put his head down on Ivan Ivanovich's outstretched hand. He saw what had happened to his master's face; it was very pale, and there were dark circles under his eyes and stubble on his unshaven cheeks.

Ivan Ivanovich turned his head toward Beem and spoke softly and weakly: "Well? What should we do? I'm sick, Beem. It's bad. The shrapnel—it's right by my heart. It's bad, Beem."

His voice was so unusual that it upset Beem, who paced the room, scratching at the door, as if to say, "Get up, let's go out, let's go." But Ivan Ivanovich was afraid to stir. Beem sat down next to him again and whimpered softly.

"Well, Beem, let's give it a try." Ivan Ivanovich barely

managed to get the words out, and rose gingerly.

He sat on the bed for a while, then stood on his feet, and, holding onto the wall with one hand and his heart with the other, slowly made his way to the door. Beem walked next to him, never taking his eyes off his friend, and not wagging his tail, not once. He seemed to be saying, "Well, there, that's good. We're going; slowly, slowly, we're going."

Out on the landing, Ivan Ivanovich rang the doorbell of his neighbor's apartment, and when little Lusya answered, he said something to her. She ran back into the apartment and returned with the old woman Stepanovna. As soon as Ivan Ivanovich said the word "shrapnel" to her, she began bustling about, took him by the arm, and led him to his bed.

"You should be in bed, Ivan Ivanovich. In bed. Here," she said, as she helped him lie down. "Just lie there. That's the only thing to do." She picked up the keys from his desk and hurried out, almost at a run, but shuffling like an old person.

Naturally, Beem took the order to lie there personally. He lay down by the bed, without taking his eyes from the door. His master's sorry state, Stepanovna's anxiety, and the fact that she took the keys—all this affected him, and he was excited.

Soon he heard the key in the door, the lock clicking, the door opening, and conversation in the vestibule. Stepanovna came in, accompanied by three strangers in white coats—two women and a man. They didn't smell like other people; they seemed to smell of the box on the wall that his master opened only when he said, "I'm not well, Beem, not well. I'm sick, boy."

The man strode confidently toward the bed, but—

Beem pounced on him, placing his front paws on his chest, and barked twice with all his might.

"Out! Out!" Beem shouted.

The man lurched back, pushing Beem away, the women ran out into the vestibule, and Beem sat down by the bed, trembling all over and prepared to die before he would let strangers

50

near his friend at such a difficult moment in his life.

The doctor said from the doorway, "Some dog! What should we do?"

Ivan Ivanovich beckoned to Beem and patted his head, turning slightly. Beem cuddled up to his friend's shoulder, licking his neck, his face, his hands.

"Come here," Ivan Ivanovich said softly, looking at the doctor.

He did.

"Give me your hand."

He did.

"Hello."

"Hello," said the doctor.

Beem touched the doctor's hand with his nose, which signified in dog language, "Well, what can you do. So be it; any friend of my friend is a friend of mine."

They brought in the stretcher. They put Ivan Ivanovich on it. He said, "Stepanovna . . . look after Beem, please, dear. Let him out in the morning. He'll come back quickly on his own. . . . Beem will wait for me." And he turned to Beem. "Wait. . . . wait. . . ."

Beem knew the word "wait." In front of the store: "Sit, wait." By the knapsack in the woods. "Sit, wait." And now he squealed and wagged his tail, which meant: "Oh, my friend will come back! He's leaving, but he'll be back soon."

Only Ivan Ivanovich understood; the others didn't—Beem could see that in their eyes. Beem sat by the stretcher and put his paw on it. Ivan Ivanovich squeezed it. "Wait, boy. Wait."

Beem had never seen this happen to his friend before, to have water flow in buckets from his eyes.

When the stretcher was gone and the door locked, he lay down by the door, stretched out his front paws and resting his cheek on the floor; that's how dogs lie when they are sad or in pain, and that's the position in which they most frequently die.

51

But Beem didn't die of sadness, like that seeing-eye dog that had lived with a blind man for many years. That dog lay down on her master's grave, refused food brought by the kind people at the cemetery, and, on the fifth day, when the sun came up, she died. And that really happened, it's not a made-up story.

No, Beem didn't die. Beem had been clearly told to wait. He believed that his friend would return. It had been that way many times; Ivan Ivanovich would say "wait" and he would return.

Wait! Now that was Beem's only goal in life.

But it was so hard, so painful, being alone that night. Something was wrong, different. Those white coats reeked of trouble. And Beem grew sadder.

At midnight, when the moon rose, it became unbearable. It made him nervous even when he was with his master, that moon; it has eyes, and it watches with those dead eyes, and glows with its dead, cold light, and Beem would hide from it in a dark corner. And now—one look from the moon sent shivers down his spine, and his master was not there to protect him. And he howled in the night, a long, resounding howl, a premonition of disaster. He was sure that someone would hear, perhaps his master.

Stepanovna came in.

"Well, Beem, what's the matter? What? Ivan Ivanovich is gone. Tsk, tsk, it's too bad."

Beem didn't reply with either a look or a tail wag. He went on staring at the door. Stepanovna turned on the lights and left. It was better with the light on—the moon moved back and seemed smaller. Beem settled down right under the light bulb, his back to the moon, but soon was back by the door, waiting.

In the morning, Stepanovna brought some cereal for Beem and put it in his bowl, but he didn't even get up. Just like the seeing-eye dog—she couldn't be roused by food, either.

"Just look how loving he is. He can't understand this. Well, go out for a walk, Beem." She opened the door. "Go play."

Beem looked up and gave the old woman a careful look. He knew the word "walk" meant freedom and "go out for a walk" meant total freedom. And Beem knew well what freedom was —do anything your master lets you. But he wasn't here, and they were telling Beem to go for a walk. What kind of freedom was that?

Stepanovna didn't know how to deal with dogs, didn't know that dogs like Beem understood people without words, and that the words they did know were full of meaning but that the meaning could change with the circumstances. So, in her naïveté, she said, "If you don't want cereal, *go seek* something else. You like grass. And maybe you'll find something in the garbage you'll like (she was too naive to know that Beem would never touch a garbage can). *Go seek.*"

Beem got up, shaking himself out. What was this? "Seek?" Seek what? "Seek" means go look for a hidden piece of cheese, look for a lost or hidden thing. "Seek" is an order, and it was Beem who determined what he had to seek, depending on the circumstances. What was there to seek now?

He said all this to Stepanovna with his eyes, his tail, with the questioning padding of his forepaws, but she didn't understand a thing, and repeated, "Go out for a walk. Seek!"

And Beem rushed out the door. He rushed down the stairs from the second floor and out into the yard. He was going to seek his master! That's what he had to seek—there was nothing else. That's how he understood things. Here's where the stretcher had stood. Yes, right here. And here were the very weak traces of the people in white coats. And the traces of a car. Beem made a circle, entered it (any half-witted dog would have done the same), but he still got the same trail. He followed it out into the street and immediately lost it by the corner: the whole roadway smelled of rubber out there. There were many different human trails, but all the car trails had blended into one. But the one he needed went from the yard out and around the corner, and so that was where he had to go.

Beem ran down one street, then another, came back to the house, checked all the places where he used to walk with Ivan Ivanovich—and there were no clues, none at all. Once he glimpsed a checked cap from a distance, and he caught up with the man—no, it wasn't the right one. He looked around carefully and established the fact that many, many people were walking around in checked caps. How was he supposed to know that this fall they were selling only checked caps and that therefore everyone liked them. He hadn't noticed it before because dogs always pay attention to (and memorize) the bottom part of people's clothing. This goes back to the wolf, to nature, for many centuries. Thus, a fox will not notice a man standing waist-high behind bushes as long as he doesn't stir and the wind doesn't carry his scent. And Beem made some sense out of it all —there was no point in seeking his master on top, because heads can all look alike in color.

The day was a clear one. Some streets had patches of leaves, others were thickly carpeted with them, so that if there had even been a tiny part of his master's scent, Beem would have found it. But there was nothing.

By midday, Beem was in despair. And suddenly in a courtyard he stumbled on the scent of the stretcher. It had been here. And then a current of that smell came at him from one side. Beem followed it like a path. The threshold smelled of the people in white coats. Beem scratched at the door. A girl dressed in a white coat opened the door and jumped back in fear. But Beem greeted her politely, asking, "Would Ivan Ivanovich be here?"

"Get out! Get out of here!" she shouted and shut the door. Then she opened it a crack and called to someone, "Petrov! Chase that mutt, or the boss will let me have it. He'll scream that I'm turning a first-aid station into a kennel! Chase him away!"

54

A man in a black jacket came from the garage, stamped his feet at Beem, and shouted without any anger at all, simply because it was his job and no hard feelings, please.

"I'll show you, you critter! Get! Get!"

Beem didn't know words like "boss," "let me have it," "kennel," "chase," or, certainly, "first-aid," but "get out!" combined with the tone of voice and mood were obvious to him. You couldn't fool Beem there. He ran off and sat down at a distance, staring at the door. If the people had known what Beem was looking for, they would have helped him, even though Ivan Ivanovich hadn't been brought here but had been taken straight to the hospital. But what can you do if dogs understand people and people can't always understand dogs or even each other? Beem himself was of course not capable of such deep thoughts, but neither could he understand why they weren't letting him through the door at which he was scratching so trustfully and straightforwardly and behind which, in all probability, lay his friend.

Beem sat under a fading lilac bush until nightfall. Cars drove up, and people in white coats got out of them, leading other people or helping them along; once in a while they would bring people out on stretchers, and then Beem would move closer to check the scent—no, not him. By evening a few had noticed the dog. Someone brought him a piece of sausage—Beem didn't touch it. Someone tried to take him by the collar—Beem ran off. Even the fellow in the black jacket walked by a couple of times and stopped to give Beem a sympathetic look and didn't stamp his feet. But Beem sat like a statue and didn't say anything to anyone. He waited.

At twilight he had a thought: What if his master was home? And he ran swiftly.

A beautiful, well-groomed dog with a shiny coat—white with a black ear—ran through the city. Every good citizen on the street would have said, "What a sweet hunting dog!"

55

Beem scratched at his own door, but it didn't open. Then he curled up on the doormat. He didn't want to eat or drink; he didn't want anything. He was depressed.

Stepanovna came out on the landing. "You're back, you poor thing?"

Beem wagged his tail once. ("I'm back.")

"Well, now have some supper." She moved his dish with the morning's cereal over to him.

Beem didn't touch it.

"I knew it. You fed yourself. Smart doggie. Sleep now." And she shut the door behind her.

That night Beem didn't howl. But he didn't leave the door—he waited.

And in the morning he became worried again. He had to seek, seek his friend! That was his whole life. And when Stepanovna let him out, he ran over to visit the people in the white coats first. But there was some fat man there this time, yelling at everybody, using the word "dog" a lot. They threw stones at Beem, purposely off-target, and waved sticks at him. Finally they lashed him very painfully with a long, flexible branch. Beem ran off a little way, sat down, waited for a while, and then appeared to decide—his friend couldn't be here, or they wouldn't be chasing him off so cruelly. And Beem left, his head down.

A sad, lonely dog walked through the city, hurt for no good reason.

He turned onto a busy street. There was an endless stream of people flowing somewhere and flowing endlessly, and they were all in a hurry and exchanging hurried words. Beem may have thought: Maybe he'll walk by here? And without any more logic to it than that, he sat down in the shade on the corner, not far from a gate, and watched the crowd, checking almost every person who went by.

First of all, Beem noticed that all people smelled of automobile exhaust, and the other smells broke through with varying success.

Here came a tall, thin man in big, worn shoes, carrying potatoes in a net bag, the same kind that his master used to carry. The thin man was carrying potatoes, but he smelled of tobacco. He was walking fast, as though trying to catch up with someone. But it only seemed that way—they were all catching up with someone. And they were all looking for something; it looked like field exercises—otherwise why were they running down the street, into doorways, and then running out again?

"Hello, Black Ear!" the thin man said as he went past.

"Hello," Beem replied glumly, moving his tail along the ground without losing his concentration and watching the crowd.

And then came a man in overalls, and he smelled like a wall when you lick it (a wet wall). He was almost all grayish-white. He was carrying a white stick with a beard on one end and a heavy bag.

"What are you doing here?" he asked Beem. "Are you settled in to wait for your master or are you lost?"

"Yes, waiting," Beem said, moving his front paws.

"So here." He took out a piece of candy from his bag and set it in front of Beem and tugged at Beem's black ear. "Eat, eat." Beem didn't touch it. "You're well trained. And intelligent. Won't eat from someone else's plate." And he went on quietly, calmly, not like everyone else.

Beem didn't know about anyone else, but as far as he was concerned, that was a good man. He knew what waiting was. He had said, "Are you waiting?" He understood Beem.

A really fat man with a fat cane, fat black-rimmed glasses approached, and carrying a fat briefcase—everything about him was fat. He smelled of papers, the kind that Ivan Ivanovich whispered on with sticks, and also, perhaps, of the yellow pieces of paper you put in your pockets. He stopped before Beem and said, "Pshaw! Well, well. What next? Dogs loose on the avenue!"

A janitor with a broom came out the gate and stood next to Fatso. Fatso went on, talking to the janitor, pointing at Beem. "Do you see? And on your property, I'll bet."

"That's a fact, I see him." And he leaned on his broom, brush side up.

"You see? You don't see a thing," Fatso replied angrily. "He won't even eat candy, he's so full. How am I expected to live with this going on?" He was really mad.

"So don't live," the janitor said and added, "Look how emaciated you are, poor fellow."

"You're insulting me!"

Three teenagers stopped and smiled, looking back and forth at Beem and Fatso.

"What are you laughing at? What's so funny? I'm telling him —a dog. A thousand dogs eating two or three kilos of meat a day —that's two or three tons a day. Do you realize how much that is?"

One of the boys objected, "Even a camel couldn't eat three kilos."

The janitor calmly corrected him, "Camels don't eat meat." Suddenly he grabbed his broom and energetically swept the pavement in front of Fatso. "Move along, citizen! Well? What did I tell you, blockhead?"

Fatso left, spitting mad. The three boys also left, laughing to themselves. The janitor stopped sweeping. He patted Beem on the back, stood around for a bit, and then said, "Sit and wait. He'll come." And he went back in.

Out of the entire incident Beem not only understood the words "meat" and "dog," but he heard the voices and, more importantly, he *saw* everything, and that was enough for a smart dog to figure out that Fatso had a bad life, and the janitor a good one; one was angry and the other kind. Who would know

58

better than Beem that at the crack of dawn the streets are inhabited only by janitors and that they respect dogs. Beem even approved slightly of the fact that he chased Fatso away. In general, this silly incident only distracted Beem, but it may have served a purpose in helping him begin to realize that people were all different—they could be good and they could be bad. And perhaps that was a good thing to learn. But as far as Beem was concerned, it was totally unimportant. He didn't have time for it; he was busy watching the passersby.

Some women gave off a sharp and irritating scent, like lily-of-the-valley, those little white flowers that destroyed Beem's sense of smell; in those cases, Beem turned away and held his breath for a few seconds. He didn't like it. Most women had lips the color of the flags during the wolf roundup; Beem disliked that color, too, as did most animals, dogs and bulls in particular. Almost all the women were carrying something. Beem noticed that men with packages were less frequent than women.

And still he didn't see Ivan Ivanovich. My friend! Where are you?

People continued to flow past. Beem's depression had lessened slightly, and he stared ahead all the more attentively. Was *he* coming? Today Beem would wait here. Wait!

A man with flabby lips, thick wrinkles, a pug nose, and bulging eyes stopped in front of Beem and shouted, "Disgusting!" People began stopping. "We're surrounded by flies, epidemics, stomach cancer, and what do we have here?" He pointed his hand at Beem. "Here in a crowd of people, in the midst of our workers, sits living contagion!"

"Not every dog is contagious. Look how nice he is," said a girl.

The pug-nosed man looked her up and down and turned away in disgust. "What craziness! You are crazy, young woman!"

And then— Ah, if only Beem had been human! That woman, that "Soviet woman" from long ago—that slanderer—came

59

over. Beem was scared at first, but then, the fur bristling on his neck, he took up a defensive posture. And the woman began gabbing to the people standing in a semicircle around Beem.

"It is craziness! It bit me. Bit-i-it me-ee-e!" And she showed them all her hand.

"Where's the bite?" asked a teenager with a book bag. "Let's see."

"Insolent pup!" she said and hid her hand.

Everyone except Pug Nose laughed.

"Some upbringing you got at the institute, you devil, you. Some upbringing," she attacked the student. "You don't believe me, a Soviet woman? What will you be like when you grow up? Where are we headed, dear citizens? Or aren't we under Soviet rule anymore?"

The teenager blushed and replied, "If you knew what you looked like, you'd envy that dog." He took a step toward her. "Who gave you the right to insult me?"

Even though Beem didn't understand the words, he couldn't stand any more. He leaped in the woman's direction, barked as loud as he could, and dug all four feet into the ground, restraining himself from further action (he couldn't be held responsible for the consequences). An intelligent dog! But still, only a dog.

The woman began screeching, "Po-lice! Po-lice!"

There was a whistle, and someone came over saying, "Move along, citizens! Let's get back to our business!" It was a policeman. (Beem even wagged his tail, despite his agitation.) "Who screamed?! You?" He asked the woman.

"She did," the student confirmed.

Pug Nose stuck his nose in.

"What are you doing? What have you been doing?" He attacked the policeman. "Dogs—there are dogs on the avenue of a major city!"

"Dogs!" the woman cried.

"And Cro-Magnons like *them!*" the student shouted.

"He insulted me!" She was almost weeping.

"Citizens, move along! And you, you, and you, off to head-quarters," he said, indicating the woman, the student, and Pug Nose.

"What about the dog?" the woman squealed. "You haul off innocent people, but the dog—"

"I won't go," the student said.

A second policeman came up. "What's going on here?"

A man with a tie and hat gave a decorous, reasoned explanation, "That one there, that student type, doesn't want to go down to headquarters. He's a troublemaker. Those there, both of them, they want to, but he doesn't. Troublemaker."

Both policemen exchanged a look and took the student with them. Pug Nose and the woman traipsed after. The crowd broke up, and no one paid any attention to the dog except for the nice girl. She went up to Beem and petted him, but she also followed the police. She went on her own, Beem saw. He followed her with his eyes, then shuffled his feet and ran after her and walked alongside.

The girl and the dog were walking to headquarters.

"Whom were you waiting for, Black Ear?" she asked.

Beem sat down gloomily, lowering his head.

"And your stomach looks rather empty, dearie. I'll feed you; you just wait, Black Ear, I'll feed you."

Beem had been called Black Ear several times now. And his master used to say, "Hey you, Black Ear!" He had said that a long, long time ago, when Beem was a baby. Where is my friend? thought Beem. And he went on with the girl, deeply depressed.

They entered headquarters together. The woman was screaming there, and the pug-nosed man was roaring. The student, head hung low, was silent, and a strange policeman sat behind a desk, giving all three an unfriendly look.

The girl said, "I've brought in the guilty party." And pointed

61

at Beem. "He's a nice dog. I saw everything and heard it all from the very beginning. This guy"—she nodded in the student's direction—"isn't at fault in any way."

She told the story calmly, sometimes pointing at Beem, sometimes at one of the three. They tried to interrupt her, but the policeman stopped the woman and Pug Nose. He obviously was well disposed toward the girl. She finished up with a joking question to Beem: "Am I telling it right, Black Ear?" And, turning to the policeman, she added, "My name is Dasha." And then to Beem: "I'm Dasha. Understand?"

Beem used his whole body to show that he did.

"Here, come here, Black Ear. Here!" the policeman said.

Oh, Beem knew that word. For sure. And he came over.

The policeman patted him lightly on the neck, looked at his collar, checked the number, and wrote it down. And he told Beem to lie down.

Beem obeyed; hind legs tucked in, front extended, head cocked, and eyes fixed on his interlocutor.

The policeman was on the phone.

"Hunter's Society?"

"Hunting?" Beem shuddered. "Hunting!" What could it mean here?

"Hunter's Society. The police calling. Check number twenty-four. A setter. What do you mean you don't have it? That's impossible. It's a good dog, well trained. Check City Hall? All right." He hung up and redialed, talked, asked questions, and wrote things down, repeating them as he did: "Setter—with external inherited flaws, no pedigree certificate, owner Ivan Ivanovich Ivanov, Forty-one Proezzhaya Street. Thanks." Now he turned to the girl. "You are terrific, Dasha. You found his master."

Beem jumped up, touching the policeman's knee with his nose, licked Dasha's hand, and looked into her eyes, straight into her eyes, the way only wise and gentle dogs can look. He

62

had understood that they were talking about Ivan Ivanovich, his friend, his brother, his god. And he was trembling with excitement.

The policeman spoke curtly to the woman and Pug Nose. "Go on. Good-bye."

Pug Nose started berating the policeman: "That's it? What kind of law and order is this? You're too lax!"

"Go on, go on, pops. Good-bye. Get a rest."

"What do you mean, 'pops'? How dare you? You've even forgotten how to be polite, you jerks. And you want to bring up people like that," he said, pointing at the student, "patting them on the head. Go on. Just wait; one day he'll turn on you, and then it'll be too late. Woof! He'll eat you up." His bark was very authentic.

Beem, naturally, replied in kind.

The policeman laughed. "Watch it, pops. The dog understands, and it's taking sides."

The woman jumped at both barks and backed toward the door, shouting, "It's barking at me, at me! And in a police station, too—there's no protection anywhere for a Soviet woman."

They finally left.

"And are you holding me?" the student demanded.

"You must obey, young man. If you're asked down to the station, you have to go. That's the law."

"The law? There's no law that says you can drag a sober citizen down to the station like a thief. The woman should have gotten fifteen days, and you just— Ah!" Then he left, giving Beem's ear a friendly tweak on the way out.

Beem didn't understand anything anymore. Bad people yell at the policeman, and good ones do, too, and the policeman takes it all and even chuckles. It was more than a smart dog could figure out.

"You'll take him yourself?" the policeman asked Dasha.

"Yes. Home, Black Ear, we're going home."

Beem walked in front now, looking back at Dasha and waiting for her. He knew the word "home," and that's just where he was leading her. The other people hadn't figured out that he would have gone back to the apartment on his own, anyway; they thought that he was a dumb dog. Only Dasha understood, only Dasha—that blond girl with the big, dreamy, warm eyes, which Beem believed in the moment he looked into them. And he brought her to his door. She rang—no answer. She rang again, at the neighbor's door. Stepanovna came out. Beem greeted her. He was much cheerier than he had been yesterday. He was saying, "Here's Dasha. I brought Dasha." (There was no other explanation for the looks Beem gave Stepanovna and Dasha.)

The women talked quietly, saying "Ivan Ivanovich" and "shrapnel"; then Stepanovna unlocked the door. Beem invited Dasha in, never taking his eyes from her. She picked up his bowl and sniffed it.

"It's sour." She threw out the cereal, washed the bowl, and put it back on the floor. "I'll be right back; wait for me, Black Ear."

"His name is Beem," Stepanovna told her.

Stepanovna took a chair. Beem sat down in front of her, but he kept looking at the door.

"You're a quick dog," Stepanovna said. "You've been left all alone, but you know who likes you. So do I, Beem. I'm living with my granddaughter in my declining years. After she was born, her parents applied for jobs in Siberia, and so I'm bringing her up. And she loves me, my granddaughter, she loves me best. She's good to me."

Stepanovna poured out her heart for her own sake while addressing Beem. People sometimes talk to dogs, or a favorite horse, or a cow, when they have no one else to talk to. And smart dogs easily recognize an unhappy person and always express their sympathy. But Beem was suffering because the people in white coats had taken his friend away. All the unpleasant events of the day had merely deflected his pain, and now it returned in full force. He heard the familiar words "good" and "to me" spoken with sorrowful warmth. So, naturally, he came closer and placed his head on Stepanovna's knee, and she dabbed at her eyes with a hankie.

Dasha returned with a package. Beem came up to her, lay flat on the floor, putting one paw on her shoe and his head on the other paw. That was his way of saying "Thank you."

Dasha got two meat patties and two boiled potatoes from the bag and put them in his bowl.

"Here."

Beem didn't eat, even though it was the third day since he'd had even a crumb in his mouth. Dasha was rubbing his ruff gently and coaxing him, "Take it, Beem, take it."

Dasha had a soft, soulful, gentle voice, and a calm one; her hands were warm and gentle, too. But Beem turned away from the meat. Dasha opened Beem's mouth and pushed in a pattie. Beem held it in his mouth, staring at Dasha in surprise, and the meat went down on its own. The same thing happened with the second one. And with the potatoes.

"You have to force-feed him," Dasha told Stepanovna. "He's pining for his master; that's why he's not eating."

"Don't be silly! A dog will find its own food. Look at all the strays—they manage to eat."

"What should we do?" Dasha asked Beem. "You'll just die like this."

"No, he won't," Stepanovna said positively. "A smart dog like that won't. I'll make him a stew every day. He's a living creature; I'll take care of him."

Dasha thought about something and then removed his collar.

"Don't let him out until I come back with his collar. I'll be here around ten tomorrow morning. But where is Ivan Ivanovich now?"

Beem perked up; they were talking about *him!*

65

"They flew him to Moscow. The heart surgery is complicated. The shrapnel fragment is right next to it."

Beem was all attention: "shrapnel," again that "shrapnel." The word sounded like sorrow. But if they were talking about Ivan Ivanovich, that meant that he was somewhere. He had to seek him. Seek!

Dasha left. So did Stepanovna. Beem was left to pass the night alone once more. He would doze off for a few minutes. And each time he dreamed about Ivan Ivanovich—at home or hunting in the woods. And then he would jump up, looking around, pacing the room, sniffing the corners, listening in the silence, and lying down by the door. The welt raised by the lashing that morning hurt terribly, but that was nothing compared to his great sorrow and uncertainty.

Wait. Wait. He had to grit his teeth and wait.

7

THE SEARCH CONTINUES

Beem was almost in tears the next morning. The sun was above the window, and still no one had come. He listened to the footsteps of the tenants as they walked past his door from higher floors or came upstairs. All the footsteps were familiar, but *his* weren't among them. Finally he heard Dasha's step. Dasha! Beem let her know he was there. In translation his cry meant: "I hear you, Dasha!"

"Just a minute," she said and rang Stepanovna's doorbell.

They came into Beem's apartment. He greeted each woman, and then ran over to the door and stood there, looking back at them, asking, with a pleading wag of the tail, "Open up. It's time to go seek."

Dasha put on his collar. It now sported a bright yellow plastic tag imprinted with the following: "His name is Beem. He's waiting for his master. He knows how to get home. He lives alone in the apartment. Don't hurt him, people." Dasha read the sign to Stepanovna.

"What a kind soul you are! You must love dogs, eh?"

Dasha petted Beem and said, "My husband left me, my son died. And I'm only thirty. I had an apartment here. I'm moving away."

"All alone. Oh, you poor dear darling." Stepanovna clucked over her. "Why that's just—"

But Dasha cut her off. "I have to go." At the door she added, "Don't let Beem out for a while or he'll just follow me."

Beem tried to squeeze out the door with Dasha, but she pushed him back and left with Stepanovna.

A hour later, Beem began whining, and then howled with such longing in his voice, howled the way people mean when they say, "I feel like howling like a dog," that Stepanovna let him out. (Dasha was far away by now.) "Well, go on. I'll have stew for you in the evening."

Beem paid no attention to her words or her eyes; he raced down the stairs and out into the court. He cast in the courtyard and then went out on the street. After standing still, thinking a bit, he began reading the smells line after line, disregarding even those trees that had been signed by his brothers.

Beem uncovered no traces of Ivan Ivanovich that day. By evening, just to make sure, he wandered into a park in a new part of town. Four boys were playing ball. He sat for a bit, checking out the surroundings, as much as his nose would let him, and was about to leave. But a boy of twelve or so stopped playing and came over to look curiously at him.

"Who do you belong to?" he asked, as though Beem could tell him.

First of all, Beem said hello—he wagged his tail, but sadly, cocking his head first to one side and then the other. This also served to ask the question: "And you—what kind of a person are you?"

The boy realized that the dog didn't trust him completely, and he came over confidently and extended his hand, "Hello, Black Ear."

When Beem gave him his paw, the boy called out, "Hey, fellas! Come here!"

His friends ran over but stopped at a safe distance.

"Look at how wise his eyes are!" the first boy exclaimed.

"Maybe he's a trained dog?" a tubby little fellow suggested

reasonably. "Tolya, tell him to do something—see if he understands."

A third boy, somewhat older than the rest, pronounced au-
thoritatively, "It's trained. See, it's wearing a tag."

"It couldn't be trained," a thin boy countered. "It wouldn't
be so skinny and droopy if it were."

Beem really had lost a lot of weight and his former good looks
—his stomach had contracted, his unkempt fur was matted on
his flanks and dull on his once-shiny back. Depression and hunger were taking their toll.

Tolik touched Beem's forehead, and the dog looked at all the
boys and expressed his total trust. After that, they all took turns
petting him, and he didn't mind. Tolik read the tag aloud.

"He's Beem! And lives all alone! Fellas, he's hungry. Quick,
run home and come back with whatever you can get."

Beem stayed with Tolik, and the other boys ran off. The boy
sat on a bench, and Beem lay at his feet and sighed deeply.

"It's tough for you, isn't it, Beem?" Tolik asked, petting him
on the head. "Where's your master?"

Beem pressed his nose against Tolik's shoe and lay there. Soon
the boys came back. Tubby brought a meat pie; Grown-up, a
piece of sausage; Skinny, two pancakes. They put it all in front
of Beem, but he didn't even sniff it.

"He's sick," said Skinny. "Maybe even contagious." And he
backed off from Beem.

Tubby wiped his hands on his shorts and also moved away.
Grown-up rubbed the sausage in Beem's nose and concluded
confidently, "He won't eat. He doesn't want to."

"Mama says all dogs are contagious," Tubby worried, "and
this one is really sick."

"Well, then, leave!" Tolik muttered angrily. "I don't want to
see a trace of you here! 'Contagious!' The dog catchers get the
contagious ones. This one even has a tag."

His reasonable argument convinced them; they again

crowded around Beem. Tolik pulled his collar, and Beem sat up. Tolik pulled back Beem's soft lip and saw an opening in his jaw, in the back where the teeth end; he tore off a piece of sausage and pushed it into the opening—Beem swallowed. Another piece—another swallow. And he polished off the sausage to their general approval. They all watched closely, and Tubby swallowed along with Beem, even though he had nothing in his mouth—he was helping Beem. Tolik couldn't push in pieces of the meat pies, because they crumbled, but Beem took a pie, lay down on his stomach, placed the pie on his paws, looked at it for a while, and then ate it. He obviously did it out of respect for Tolik's feelings. The boy had such gentle hands and such soft, slightly sad eyes, and he pitied Beem so much that the dog couldn't resist. He ate the pie for Tolik, and that was that. And he began to feel better, because he didn't refuse the pancakes, either. It was only his second meal in a whole week.

Tolik spoke first after Beem's repast. "Let's find out what tricks he knows."

Skinny said, "In the circus when they want the dogs to jump, they yell, *'Up!'* "

Beem sat up and looked at the boy intently, as if asking, "Up —over what?"

Two of them held a belt taut, and Tolik ordered, "Beem! Up!"

Beem jumped easily over the simple barrier. The boys were overjoyed. Tubby ordered, "Lie!"

Beem lay down. (Please, anything you ask, with pleasure!)

"Sit," Tolik asked. (Beem sat.) "Fetch!" He threw his cap.

Beem brought back the cap. Tolik hugged him, and Beem on his part returned the affection with a wet lick on the cheek.

Of course, Beem felt much better with these children. But a man came over, twirling a cane, came over so quietly that the children didn't even notice him until he asked, "Whose dog?"

He looked important, in a gray, narrow-brimmed hat, gray bow tie, gray suit, and with a gray beard and glasses. Without

70

taking his eyes off Beem, he repeated, "Whose dog is this, boys?"

Grown-up and Tolik answered simultaneously.

"No one's," said one naively.

"Mine," said Tolik guardedly. "At this moment, it's mine."

Tolik had seen the Gray Man several times; he strolled alone around the park self-importantly. One time he had a dog that held back and didn't want to go with him. And once he came over to the children and lectured them; he said that they didn't know how to play as in the olden days, and that they were disrespectful, and that they were brought up wrong, not like the olden days, and that people had fought for them back in the Civil War, for children just like them, and that they didn't appreciate it, and that they didn't know how to do anything, and that they should be ashamed of themselves.

That day when the Gray Man lectured them, Tolik was nine. Now he was twelve. But he remembered the man. Tolik sat hugging Beem and said, "Mine."

"Well, which is it—no one's or his?" the man asked the others.

"There's a tag on it." Tubby put in his two cents' worth at the wrong time.

The Gray Man petted Beem's ear and read his collar.

Beem sensed definitely—absolutely for sure—that the Gray Man gave off the scent of dogs. It was distant, a few days old, but it was there. He looked into his eyes and immediately distrusted him—he didn't trust his voice, his eyes, not even his scent. It couldn't be that the man had just collected the distant scents of various dogs for nothing. Beem huddled closer to Tolik, trying to get free of the Gray Man, but the man wouldn't let go.

"You shouldn't lie, child," the man said. "According to the tag, it's not your dog. Shame on you. Have your parents taught you to lie? What will you be like when you've grown up? Oh dear, tsk-tsk-tsk!" He took a leash out of his pocket and attached it to Beem's collar.

71

Tolik grabbed the leash and shouted, "Don't touch him! I won't let you!"

The Gray Man removed Tolik's hand.

"I'm obliged to return the dog to the place indicated. Perhaps there'll be a report to fill out." (He pronounced it rEE-port). "Perhaps his owner is a victim of al-CO-hol. If so, the dog will have to be taken away from him. That's my duty, to do things honestly and humanely. That's the way. I'll find its apartment and check to see that everything is in order."

"You don't believe the tag?" Tolik demanded stubbornly, almost in tears.

"I believe it, child, I believe it. But—" He raised his index finger and declaimed didactically, almost solemnly, "Trust, but check!" And he led Beem away.

Beem hung back, looking back at Tolik. He saw that the boy was crying but—what can you do!—he went with Gray Man, tail tucked in and eyes on the ground, not himself at all. His whole manner seemed to say, "That's what happens with your master gone." All he had to do was bite him in the calf and run away, but Beem was an intelligent dog and he went where he was led.

They went down a street where all the buildings were new. All new. And all were gray and so similar that even Beem could have gotten lost in them. In one of the buildings they went up to the third floor, and Beem noted that all the doors were the same, too.

A woman in a gray dress opened the door.

"Another one! Oh, good grief!"

"Shut up!" Gray Man took off Beem's collar and showed it to her. The woman put on her glasses and started to read it. He went on, "You just don't appreciate me. I'm the only collector of dog tags in the entire republic. And that tag is really something! It's my five hundredth!"

Beem didn't understand a thing—nothing—there wasn't a

familiar word or an understandable gesture. Nothing.

Gray Man went into a room with the collar in his hand. He called out, "Beem, come here!"

Beem thought about it and carefully went in. He looked around from the threshold and sat down there. One clean wall was hung with velvet-covered boards with row upon row of dog tags: numbers, disks, gray and yellow medallions, several red leashes and collars, several muzzles and other pieces of dog equipment, including a nylon choking cord, which Beem, of course, did not recognize as such—even a human would have been mystified by it, but as far as Beem was concerned it was just a rope.

Beem watched attentively while Gray Man worked on his collar, removing the tag with pliers and attaching it to the center of one of the boards; he did the same thing with his license number and then put Beem's collar back on.

"You're a good dog," he said.

His master used to say just that, but this time Beem didn't believe it. He went out to the vestibule and stood in front of the door, saying, "Let me out! There's nothing for me here."

"Let him out," the woman said. "What did you drag him here for, anyway? You could have removed the tags out on the street."

"I couldn't—the kids were hanging around. And I can't let him out now, either. They'll see he's missing the tags, and they might make trouble. So he'll sleep here until dawn. Lie down!"

Beem lay down by the door. What else could he do? And yet, if he had howled, run around the apartment, and attacked Gray Man, they would have let him out. But Beem knew how to wait. And he was tired. He was so weak that he actually fell asleep in front of a stranger's door, even though it was a troubled sleep.

It was the first night that Beem hadn't come home to his own apartment. He sensed it when he woke up and couldn't understand where he was. And when he did, he grew sad. He had dreamed about Ivan Ivanovich again; he dreamed about him every time he fell asleep, and, on awaking, felt the warmth of his hands, so familiar since his puppyhood. Where is he, my good and kind friend? Where? The pain was unbearable. He was so lonely, and there was nowhere to go to get away from it. And Gray Man was snoring like a hare being chased by a borzoi. And all those velvet boards smelled of dead dogs. Misery. And Beem began whimpering. And then he barked twice, with a howling whimper, like a hound when it finds a hare's trail. Finally he couldn't stand it anymore and began howling.

"Oh-oh-ow! Ow-ow-ow, people," he cried. "I'm so sad, it's so sad without my master. Let me out, let me go look for him. Ow-ow-ow, people, ow!"

Gray Man jumped up, turned on the light, and started beating Beem with a stick.

"Quiet, shut up, you! The neighbors will hear. Take that! Take that!"

Beem dodged the blows, instinctively protecting his head, and moaned like a human being, "Oh—aah—ahhgr—oh."

But the evil man managed to land a blow on his head. Beem blacked out for a few seconds, his legs twitching, but he came to quickly, leaped away from the door, backed into a corner, and bared his teeth. For the first time.

Gray Man backed off from Beem.

"Aha! He's going to bite me, the devil!" He opened the door.

But Beem didn't believe that the door was really open, and he didn't believe it when Gray Man said, "Go on, go on. Go for a walk, Beem. Go, little doggie, go on."

He didn't trust that friendly, ingratiating tone, the flattery after the beating. Flattery after a beating—that was a new discovery for Beem. The woman and Pug Nose were simply bad people. But this one— Beem hated this one. Hated him! Beem was beginning to lose his faith in man. Yes, that was what was happening.

Beem stretched his neck, snarled, and moved on Gray Man, quietly but with determination, slowly but surely. Gray Man flattened himself against the wall.

"What's the matter with you? What are you doing?"

The woman in her nightgown shouted at the man, "See? You've done it now! He's going to bite you!"

Beem saw that the horrible man was afraid of him, deathly afraid of him. This strengthened Beem's resolve. He jumped, bit his dodging enemy in a soft spot, and dashed out the open door. Beem ran with the taste of a human backside in his mouth, a backside he hated with every fiber of his being. No, Beem didn't consider himself pathetic and miserable. No, he was brave now, and bravery always goes hand in hand with pride and a sense of self-worth—even in a skunk.

Beem ran down the street in the predawn murkiness, wearing his collar, but without the "24." At first he headed in the wrong direction—that is, out of town (there were no more houses). He came back and found himself in the labyrinth of identical houses. He circled and turned until he came on the house he had escaped from. He then found the right direction, aided by something humans know little about—yesterday when he was brought here he had noticed the signature of a brother on one corner and of another brother on a second one; and now, running from one signature to the other, he got the right orientation.

By daylight he was home, upstairs, and scratching at his own door. There was no answer. He scratched again. Still no answer. And, more important, there was no trace of Ivan Ivanovich by the door. And it was too early for Stepanovna to hear Beem's call. He sat pensively on the doorstep.

He ached all over from the beating, his head was pounding, he felt nausea, and he had no strength left. But still he went out again. He went out to look for his friend. Who but Beem would look for him?

A despondent-looking dog roamed the city, a dog that was loyal, faithful, and brave.

8

AN INCIDENT AT THE RAILROAD

Days passed. Beem didn't notice anymore. He searched the city and grew to know all its nooks. Now he followed a certain route; if people had known, they would have been able to set their watches by him. If he was at the park, it was five in the morning; at the train station, it was six; at the factory, seven-thirty; at the prospect, noon; at the left bank, four in the afternoon; and so on.

And Beem made new friends among people. He had found out that most of them were good, and they were the ones who walked down the street in silence, while the bad ones always babbled a lot. He found men who smelled of oil and iron (he had encountered one or two before). They poured through the gates and into a building promptly at eight in the morning. They were as noisy as rooks, and it was hard to tell what they were saying, but Beem didn't really care. He would sit to one side of the stream of people and wait.

"Hey! Black Ear! Greetings!" A man in blue overalls always greeted him that way and set a package of food in front of him. "Still alive, fellow? Hello." And he would offer Beem his kind hand, rough but warm.

Others would shake hands wordlessly with Beem, and hurry on. No one here ever hurt him.

Beem was learning to classify people. For instance, he often ran into a buxom woman with fat legs, who was always happy and peppy; but as soon as she saw Beem, she spat like a cat, clutching her well-filled shopping bag to her chest, and said the same thing, "How disgusting! Can't all these dogs be put to sleep so that they don't get on people's nerves? Some slogan we have: 'My police force protects me.' Hah! Some protection! A dog can wander up to you in broad daylight and pull off your skirt. What do the police care? They need us as much as a dog needs a fifth leg!"

Since she always said the same thing, Beem, in his simplicity, assumed that was the woman's name—Fifth Leg. He knew for sure: Keep away from her. It didn't matter that the only words he understood were her name, but he could hear and see, and he made it a rule to avoid people like her. And then he began determining (sensing, probably) who was to be avoided. The good people were a vast majority, and the bad ones individual occurrences, but all the good people were afraid of the bad ones. His understanding of people was deepening, and from a dog's point of view he was no longer wet behind the ears, a dilettante and idealist ready to wag his tail for anyone. In a short time, Beem had become a skinny and serious dog, and he had only one aim in life—to seek and wait.

And so, early one morning, checking the scents on a sidewalk, he reeled with joy. He stopped, snorted, and ran off like a mad dog, as though he were seeing and hearing nothing. At least that's how it looked to passersby. Actually, he was following a fresh scent: Dasha had walked here! Very recently.

The trail led to the railroad station. It was impossible to get inside the building; there were people everywhere, pushing and shoving outside some window on the street, huffing and puffing, screaming like dogs that had caught a rabbit and were tearing it to shreds, disobeying the horn and the whip. It was also impossible to keep track of Dasha's scent—it had vanished. Beem circled the station and ended up on the platform. There, people were standing in front of the doors of long houses on wheels, and they weren't pushing or screaming, but were hugging, kissing, and even dancing in place. No one had any interest in Beem, and so he moved about freely between people's legs and concentrated on reading the platform.

And he smelled Dasha in front of one of the doors. Beem started for the steps, but a woman with a big badge on her chest chased him away. He didn't give up, he began sniffing the windows and peering into them. Then he noticed that two women in white coats were the last to enter the house where he'd smelled Dasha. He rushed toward them, but the house started moving slowly. Beem ran for the windows. His dog brain had come to a perfectly natural conclusion: Dasha was there, people in white coats were there, therefore Ivan Ivanovich could also be there. He could! Perhaps the people in white coats were taking him away?

And so Beem, poor Beem, miserable Beem, ran alongside the house, looking into the windows. And Dasha saw him.

"Beem! Bee-eem!" she called. "Darling Beem! You came to see me off! My sweet Beem! Bee-eem! Bee-ee—"

Her voice grew fainter and fainter. The house was getting away. No matter how Beem tried and how hard he ran, he fell farther and farther behind.

He kept running after the last house until it disappeared from view, ran on even after that, down the same road, since it didn't turn off anywhere. He ran for a long time. And finally, barely breathing, he fell between the tracks, all four legs extended, panting and whimpering softly. There wasn't any hope left at all. He didn't want to go anywhere, and he didn't have the strength for it, anyway. He didn't want anything, not even to live.

When dogs lose hope, they die naturally—quietly, without a murmur, and the world does not know how they suffer. It wasn't Beem's business to know, nor could he understand that

79

if there were no hope at all, not a single drop, all the people in the world would also die of despair. It was much simpler for Beem; it hurt so very much inside, and his friend was gone, and that was it. As the swan dies after his beloved is gone, soaring up and plummeting like a rock; as the crane that has lost its only mate spreads its wings, prostrate, and cries, begging the moon for death; so Beem lay, hallucinating about his one and only, irreplacable friend, prepared for anything and not even aware of it. But he was silent now. There isn't one person on this earth who has heard a dog die. Dogs die in silence.

Ah, if Beem could only have a few gulps of water! He would probably never have gotten up, if not for—

A woman came over to him. She was wearing a padded jacket and padded pants, and her hair was hidden by a scarf. She had apparently taken Beem for dead—she bent over him on her knees and listened for his breathing. He had grown so weak since the separation from his friend that he certainly shouldn't have tried to chase the train—that was senseless. But what does sense mean at such a time?

The woman cradled Beem's head and lifted it.

"What's the matter, doggie? What is it, Black Ear? Who were you running after, poor thing?"

The rough-looking woman had a warm, calm voice. She went down the embankment and returned with some water in her waterproof mitten. She raised Beem's head again and wet his nose in it. Beem licked the mitten. Then, his head shaking weakly, he stretched out his neck and licked again. And then he began drinking. The woman stroked his back. She understood everything: someone he loved had left forever, and it was terrible, horrible to see someone off forever—it was like burying him alive.

She confessed to Beem, "It happened to me, too. I saw my father and my husband off to war. You see, Black Ear, I'm old now, but I still can't forget. I ran after the train, too, and I fell like you and asked to die. Drink, my dear doggie, drink, you poor thing."

Beem drank almost all the water. He looked into the woman's eyes and trusted her immediately; she was a good person. And he licked her rough, cracked hands, lapping up the drops that fell from her eyes. This was the second time that Beem had tasted human tears; the first were his master's, and now these transparent tears, glistening in the sun, heavily salted by undying grief.

The woman picked him up and carried him down the embankment.

"Lie here, Black Ear. Stay. I'll be back." She went to the spot where several women were digging on the line.

Beem watched her with clouded eyes. With a great effort, he got up and followed her slowly and unsteadily. She looked back and waited for him. He reached her and lay down at her feet.

"Did your master abandon you? Is he gone?"

Beem sighed. And she understood.

They reached the women who were digging. They were all dressed like the Good Woman.

A man was standing off to one side, with a fur cap on his head and a pipe between his teeth. He spoke angrily. "Got yourself mixed up with a dog, Matryona? Who's supposed to do the work, then? What am I going to do with you?"

Beem found out that the Good Woman's name was Matryona. She ordered him to lie down on the grass; then she picked up a pair of huge tongs and clamped them onto a wooden tie with the other women.

"One-two, heave!" the man ordered. "One more time! Come on!" He shouted at them proudly, his arms akimbo.

The women heaved each time he shouted, pulling the heavy piece of lumber after them. The women's faces turned red with each heave, but the effort made one woman, a thin, spindly creature, grow pale and then turn blue. Matryona pushed her away and said in the same tone Beem's master had used when he chased him off, "Go away! Get some rest or you'll give up the ghost."

And then she spoke to the man: "Well, go on, shout, you fanatic!"

"One-two, heave!" he barked, and, readjusting his cap, he called out a work chant to keep them in rhythm: "Come on, girls, and pull that tie. Your man has told you a good-bye. He didn't get so far from you! He's married; you can cry boo-hoo! Stop! Tools down!"

Beem didn't understand any of the words.

The women put down their tongs and took up iron spikes, which they hit with long, heavy hammers. Matryona drove spikes easily, almost playfully, with three blows. The Weak One moaned with each blow.

"Come on, come on," the man hurried her on, packing his pipe. "Come on, Anisya!" He came over to her and said, "Put some power in your swing, it'll be easier."

So the Weak One was Anisya. She spent more time over each spike and fell behind the others. Something strange happened then that the women couldn't understand. Beem walked weakly to Anisya and licked her salty gloves. They all stopped work and stared at Beem in surprise.

Then, at the man's command, they sat down under the bushes to eat lunch, which each had brought. And they fed Beem. He ate. Now he would accept food from good people. That was what saved him.

By evening he grew restless. He would go up to Matryona, sit, feebly paw the ground, look into her face, go off, lie down, but soon return, and then go away again.

"You want to leave, don't you, Black Ear?" Matryona asked. "Well, go on, go, Black Ear. What would I do with you, anyway? I have no place for you. Go on."

Beem said good-bye and went off, slowly, not at all like a dog.

He followed the tracks back into town. A road is a road, it shows you where to go, you'll never go wrong when you're headed in the right direction. But his whole body ached from the beating the Gray Man had given him the day before. It was hard to breathe and walk at the same time, but—what can you do!—he had to walk. It was a good thing he had had some rest and gotten some food from the Good Woman, and that the path along the tracks was smooth and even. Gradually he got into his stride and started jogging. Dogs are full of vitality; they spring back quickly!

The sight was not an unusual one—nothing more than a sick dog wending its way along the railroad track.

Closer to town, the one road turned into two—another pair of rails stretched alongside the first one. Then there were three. Suddenly two red eyes blinked next to a signal box—left, right, left, right—jumping from side to side. All animals dislike red. For instance, a wolf is incapable of leaping over a line of red flags, and a fox surrounded by them will remain in the ring for two or three days, and sometimes more. So Beem decided to go around the enormous living red light. And suddenly something creaked underfoot.

Beem squealed in terrible pain, but he couldn't free his paw from the rails; it was trapped in a switch. He howled, "It hurts! He-e-elp!"

There were no people nearby. It wasn't the fault of people. A dog can't chew off its own foot the way a wolf does when trapped. A dog waits for help; it hopes for human help.

But what was this? Two huge, bright, white eyes lit up the road and our Beem, blinding him, moving toward him inexorably. Beem rolled up into a ball in pain and fear. And he awaited the disaster in silence. But the clattering monster with those eyes stopped some thirty feet from him, and a man jumped into the light and ran toward Beem. Another came right after him.

"How did you get caught, poor guy?" the first asked.

"What should we do?" the second asked the first.

They smelled almost like the cabdrivers Beem knew, and both wore caps with big medallions.

"We'll get it for stopping, even if we are right by the station."

"It doesn't matter now," the second man replied and headed for the switch box.

Our poor Beem realized from their voices (not their words) that they were his saviors. He heard a piercing clang from the switch box, and a minute later the vise released his paw. But Beem didn't move; he was stunned. Then the man picked him up and set him down beyond the tracks. Beem spun like a top, licking his squashed toes. And yet (dogs are so observant!) he heard voices from the windows and doors of the train; now that he was out of the blinding headlights, he could see the train in the dark; various voices were repeating the words "dog" and "hunter"—very easy words.

Beem was grateful to the good, kind people. Someone, somewhere had switched the points on the line that Beem had been following trustingly. And whoever that was didn't care that some dog caught its foot and was crippled. Whatever else happened, Beem would never ever follow railroad tracks again: he had learned and knew it just as he had known long ago as a puppy that he shouldn't walk where there were cars.

Beem hobbled along on three legs, exhausted, crippled. He stopped frequently to lick the numb and swollen toes of the injured foot, and the bleeding gradually stopped, but he went on licking until each misshapen toe was pristine. It was very painful, but there was no other way. Every dog knows—it may hurt, but you take it; it may hurt, but you lick; it may hurt, but you keep quiet.

He limped up to his doorway after midnight. No! No trace of Ivan Ivanovich. Beem wanted to scratch at the door, as usual, but discovered that it was impossible; with an injured paw he not only couldn't stand on his hind legs, he could only stand on

84

three legs or lie sprawled out. So he stuck his nose in the crack of the door and checked the smells inside; his master wasn't there. That meant he was gone for good. He stood in that position for a long time, as though holding up his weakened body with his head. Then he went to the door of Stepanovna's place and spoke desperately, "Woof!"

Stepanovna gasped when she saw him.

"Oh, how terrible! Where did that happen to you?" She unlocked the door to his apartment and went in with him. "Oh, you miserable creature, you poor, pathetic dog, what am I to do with you? And what will Ivan Ivanovich say?"

Beem had just lain down in the middle of the room, legs stretched out, but— What? "Ivan Ivanovich?" Beem raised his head, turning it toward Stepanovna with difficulty, and looked at her, never taking his eyes off her, obviously asking, "Ivan Ivanovich? Where is he?"

Stepanovna didn't know how to take care of dogs, how to feed them, how to groom them, but she did know how to pity. Perhaps it was a feeling of pity that helped her to understand Beem, to guess that the words "Ivan Ivanovich" had awakened a glimmer of hope in the sick dog.

"Yes, yes, Ivan Ivanovich," she repeated. "You wait, I'll be right back." She hurried out and returned immediately with a letter, which she brought up to Beem's nose. "See? It's a letter from Ivan Ivanovich."

Beem, poor Beem, who had died and was resurrected, who had been crushed and was rescued, sick and without an ounce of hope, Beem quivered. He buried his nose in the letter, then moved his nostrils along the edges. Yes, yes, yes—here's where *he* had moved his fingers along the envelope. When Stepanovna picked up the envelope from the floor and took the letter out of it, Beem got up with effort and stretched toward her; then she got a blank sheet of paper from the envelope and put it down in front of Beem. He wagged his tail—the sheet had the scent of Ivan Ivanovich's fingers. Yes, he had rubbed his fingers on it on purpose.

"He sent it for you," Stepanovna said. "That's what he wrote: Give the blank sheet to Beem." She pointed at the paper and said, "Ivan Ivanovich . . . Ivan Ivanovich . . ."

Beem suddenly sank to the floor and lay flat, his head on the paper. Tears rolled from his eyes. He was crying for the first time in his life. They were tears of hope, joyful tears—the best tears in the world, as good as tears of reunion and happiness.

Stepanovna was beginning to understand the dog, but she also understood that she could not manage alone. She sat by Beem for a long time and thought about her life. And she wanted to go back to the village where she was born and grew up; she was so lonely and depressed in these stone cell blocks where people spent years without meeting their neighbors. But she did have the presence of mind to give Beem water.

Oh, how he had needed that water! He pulled himself up a bit and drank thirstily, spilling the water, and then lay down once more in the same position. He shut his eyes and seemed lost to the world.

At dawn Stepanovna left, tiptoeing as though afraid to disturb a severely ill patient.

And there was only a lonely dog lying in the middle of the room.

How long he slept, Beem didn't know; perhaps several hours, perhaps days. He was awakened by a burning pain in his foot. It was day because the sun was shining. Despite his pain, he sniffed the letter. His master's scent had become weaker and more distant, but that didn't matter anymore. The important thing was that *he* existed, *he* was somewhere, and he had to be found. Beem got up, drank water from his bowl, and walked around the apartment on three legs; it hurt, but he walked and walked and walked, from the room into the vestibule and back, and then around the room. Instinct told him that if one side was numb, if it hurt, you had to walk. Soon he learned to move without hurting his squashed paw. He had to keep it up in the air instead of dragging it on the floor. That hurt less. And when Stepanovna brought him food, he greeted her with a wag of the tail, making her happy, and then he ate. And why shouldn't he eat when hope had appeared and two magic words played in his brain—"seek" and "wait."

But no matter how he begged and demanded, Stepanovna wouldn't let him out until she finally realized that Beem was a living creature and that he had to go out to relieve himself. She naturally didn't know about dogs that had died of burst bowels or suffocated from constipation if they had not been let out for more than three days.

Great humanity and kindness guided Stepanovna throughout her life. Just that. She attached the leash to Beem's collar and went out. Beem limped alongside.

In the courtyard, in a far corner, the two of them stood: an old gray-haired woman and an emaciated, lame dog—that was the picture now.

Children burst out of the doorway, hurrying to school, but several of them ran over to ask, "Granny, granny, why is Beem on three legs?"

Or, "Beemie, are you in pain? Does it hurt?"

But they had to go to school; that was a big responsibility, to go to school, the first responsibility of their lives—for their parents, their teachers, their friends. That's why they didn't linger but ran off. This was a very important event for Stepanovna and Beem, even though they didn't suspect it and went home when it was time.

They met Paltitych (Pavel Titych Rydayev) in the doorway and he said, "So that's the way it is. That's a valuable dog, and you have to take good care of it. Since its owner has entrusted you with it, then take this advice: Chain it up. Without question.

Otherwise it'll run off. You can't keep track. It'll run out the door and—it's over."

"How can you put such a smart dog on a chain?" Stepanovna asked diffidently.

"Do I have to educate you, too? Listen. Without its master and without a chain, the dog will escape. And—it's over."

"But it'll make him mean, being on a chain."

"Will you understand, you ignoramus? It'll be mean, but it'll be alive. Put it on a chain, I tell you. Those are my instructions. I'm telling you for your own good—get a chain!"

Stepanovna couldn't disobey the house chairman, and so she bought a chain for a ruble and three kopeks and took Beem into the yard on it. But at home she unhooked it from his collar and tossed it in the corner. Stepanovna was a clever woman—she had her cake and ate it, too. But, as things turned out, she took Beem out only two or three times.

9

A NEW FRIEND, FALSE RUMORS, A SECRET DENUNCIATION OF BEEM, AND AN AUTHOR'S DIGRESSION

Exchanging scraps of news at school, the children spread the following story during the very first recess. There was a dog in their yard that used to walk on four legs and now it used three, and it was really skinny and it used to be normal, and it used to be smooth and now it was messy, and it used to be happy and now it was sad, and its name was Beem. Its master had been taken to Moscow for an operation, and Granny Stepanovna was taking it out now.

The rumor reached one of the education teachers, who brought it up at a district meeting the next day. The new generation, he said, was excellent in "absorbing the idea of kindness, including compassion for all living things on earth." He supported this observation with the story of one school and its interest in some dog with a black ear, whose master was hospitalized.

For three days the teachers in all the schools in the district talked to children about compassion and kindness toward animals and how school so-and-so cared about a dog. The more prudent among them stressed that in a case like this the dog should not be rabid and that children should be cautious. The teacher in Tolik's school told the same story, with simplicity and heart-felt emotion.

"Just think, children, just think!" she said. "Some cruel man tore the dog's leg off." (That's what the rumor had become as it circulated among the teachers.) "That is unworthy of a Soviet citizen. And the poor dog with the black ear is crippled for life." She turned to the correct page in her book and went on, "And now, children, let's write a composition, short and warm-hearted, on the theme 'I Love Animals.' So that you can express yourselves clearly and don't get mixed up, here's an outline in question form."

And she wrote on the blackboard, copying from her note-book:

1. What is your dog's name?
2. Is it white, or black, or some other color?
3. Does it have pointy or floppy ears?
4. Does it have a long tail?
5. What breed is it, if this is known?
6. Is it gentle or mean?
7. Do you play with it, and if you do, how?
8. Does it bite? If it does, whom does it bite?
9. Do your parents like the dog?
10. Why do you love your dog?
11. How do you feel about other animals (chickens, geese, sheep, deer, mice, and others)?
12. Have you ever seen an elk?
13. Why do they milk cows and not elks (domestic and wild animals)?
14. Should animals be loved?

Tolik was on pins and needles; he couldn't write a thing. His voice rang out in the quiet classroom: "Anna Pavlovna, what's the dog with the black ear's name?"

The teacher looked in her book.

"Boom."

"It's Beem!" Tolik cried, exciting the whole class. "Please let me go, Anna Pavlovna. Please! I have to go look for Beem, I know him—he's very kind. Please!" He pleaded piteously, ready to kiss her hands in gratitude.

"Tolik!" Anna Pavlovna sternly chided. "You're keeping the others from their work. Sit quietly and think and write your composition."

Tolik sat down. He stared at the blank page in his notebook and saw Beem. It looked as though he were concentrating on his composition along with the rest of the class, but he had only written the title: "I Love Animals." A few minutes before the bell, he started answering the questions rapidly. He continued after the bell, and Anna Pavlovna, as usual, sat at her desk and waited patiently. Finally Tolik, grim and unhappy for some reason, put his composition in front of Anna Pavlovna. And left.

Thus, his work was the last one handed in and the first one read by Anna Pavlovna (it was on top).

Tolik had answered all the questions, and more, and his composition even included an attempt at poetry, obviously plagiarized from a popular song known to all schoolchildren. Here is his composition:

I Love Animals

His name is Beem. He's white with a black ear. The ears droop. The tail is real. He's a hunting dog, not a mutt. He's gentle. I played with him once, but some boring man took him away, some mean old man. He doesn't bite. Mama and Papa can't love him because he belongs to someone else, with a yellow tag on his collar. Why I love him, I don't know, just because. I like chickens, geese, sheep, deer, and mice, too, but I'm afraid of mice. I haven't seen an elk yet, they don't live in cities. Cows are milked so that there will be milk in the stores and so that the plan will be met. [He's retarded! thought Anna Pavlovna.] They don't milk elks because there is no elk milk in stores and no one needs it.

91

Animals should be loved and the dog is man's best friend. I've just written a song:

> The elk is good,
> The deer is good,
> The mouse is good,
> But the dog is better.

I used to have guinea pigs but Mama said they smelled up the apartment, you had to hold your nose, and she gave them away to some strange girl. But I'll find Beem, anyway, even if you didn't let me go. I'll find him, anyway. I said I will. I will. Even if you are Anna Pavlovna, I don't care.

Anna Pavlovna rolled her eyes. "He's gone over the edge! God only knows what he's thinking of! These 'still waters' . . ."

She didn't complete her thought because she was a pedagogue, and so she simply, with a sense of fulfilling her duty, gave him a D.

Tolik hurried from his own, new neighborhood to another one, an old one, to school number 35, and there he found out from the children everything he needed to know: when they had seen Beem and where he lived. To his great joy, he also found out that the leg hadn't been torn off, but dangled. And he followed the children to the house, to see Beem.

He rang the doorbell. Beem replied with a question: "Woof!" ("Who's there?")

"It's me, Tolik!" the visitor shouted. He heard Beem sniff and snort, his nose pressed to the crack in the door. "Beem, it's me, Tolik!"

Beem squealed and barked. He was shouting, "Hello, Tolik!"

And the boy understood him, he understood his first sentence in dog language.

Stepanovna heard the barking and a human voice talking to the dog and came out.

"What do you want, boy?"

"I'm here to see Beem."

He explained quickly. They went in together.

Tolik didn't recognize Beem: his ribs were sticking out, his fur was matted, he was limping—no, it couldn't be Beem. But the eyes, wise and gentle, said, "It's me, Beem." Tolik crouched and let Beem smell his head. Beem sniffed him, licked his jacket, his chin and hands, and finally rested his head on the toe of Tolik's shoe. He seemed calmer now.

Stepanovna told Tolik the whole story, even though she didn't know the boy—everything she knew about Beem and Ivan Ivanovich, but she couldn't explain how and where his paw had been crushed.

"Fate," she said. "Every dog has its own destiny, too."

She spoke calmly, though bitterly, without boasting of her age or her great experience of life, treating the boy as an equal.

"Where's his tag?" Tolik asked. "There used to be one. I read it."

"There used to be one. What's your name?"

"Tolik."

"Tolik—that's a good name. It disappeared. Someone must have taken it off."

Tolik thought, It was him, the man in gray. But he didn't say so, because he wasn't sure.

"What will I do with him?" Stepanovna said, looking at Beem. "I feel so sorry for him, and I don't know what to do for him. He should see a vegetarian."

"Veterinarian," Tolik corrected, without feeling superior to her, and answered her question. "I'll come every day after school and take him out. May I?"

And so Beem got a new friend. Tolik came every day after dinner, crossing the entire city to see Beem, and took him out into the yard, down the streets, to the park, and, to the delight of all the children, he would say proudly, "The dog is man's best friend."

And he meant it differently from what he had said in his composition, which had been written in resentment.

93

And Tolik had made up his mind—he would find that Gray Man and let him have it. He started looking for him in his own neighborhood. And one day they came face-to-face.

"Mister," Tolik asked, pushing back his cap and clasping his hands behind his back, "why did you take Beem's name tag?"

"Are you crazy, boy?" The man answered a question with another question.

"You led him away with the tag. I wasn't the only one who saw it."

"And I let him go with the tag. He bit me! You'll let a dog go when it bites like a wolf."

"You're lying, mister. Beem is a gentle dog."

"Me! Me, lie? You insolent pup! Where are your parents? Where are they? Tell me, I say!"

Gray Man was partially right. Partially. He wasn't lying about being bitten by Beem, and he had every right to be indignant, but he was lying about removing the tag. He considered Beem's bite and not the removal of the tag to be primary, and switching cause and effect is useful in winning an argument. He was convinced that he was telling the truth, and he didn't care that he wasn't telling the *whole* truth.

But Tolik was sure that Beem could not have bitten the Gray Man because the Gray Man was a person and not some rabbit or fox. And so he repeated, "You're fooling me, mister. You should be ashamed of yourself."

"Scat!" the man barked. And left, limping and sticking out his rear end. (Beem must have given him a good bite.) And he was thinking, "Those brats will go to the police to complain about me, and they'll see my collection. No, I refuse to give up my five-hundredth, my special one. It's worth twenty other tags." And he decided that the best defense was offense.

So he wrote a denunciation at home and took it over to the veterinary station. It said: "A dog was running down the street (a half-breed setter with a black ear) and bit me on the run,

94

tearing out a hunk of meat from my organism, and ran on. It ran like a rabid dog, with its tail and head low, and its eyes were bloodshot. Either you send out the dog catcher's brigade to find and destroy it, or I'll report you higher up for bureaucratism and lack of action." And so on.

The vet asked, "Where were you bitten? When? What part of town? Under what circumstances? How did it happen?"

Gray Man lied like a professional, but without imagination. The personal statement of the victim made everything clear to the doctor—he had been bitten by a stray dog on the street! He picked up the phone and called someone from the rabies section.

A few minutes later, a woman doctor drove up, lowered Gray Man's pants, looked, and asked, "How many days since the bite?"

"Ten or so," the unwilling patient replied.

"You'll get rabies in four days," the doctor declared. But since the patient didn't seem worried by the inexorable sentence, she began to have some doubts about the whole situation.

"How many months since your last bath?" she asked.

"I had a bath three Saturdays before I was bitten. I've been afraid to bathe, so that I don't get gangrene. It's a serious spot, you know."

The vet spoke up. "It sure is serious. It's as big as a TV." (He was a joker, that vet.)

"Look what you've done to yourself!" the doctor continued, taking another look at the wound. "We have to get you to the hospital right away. At once! We have to begin the series of injections against rabies—in the stomach— for six months."

"Are you off your rocker?"

"Not at all," the vet interrupted. "If you won't come quietly, we'll handle it through the police. They'll come pick you up at your house if you're so ignorant."

"Me? Ignorant? Do you know where I used to work?"

"I couldn't care less," the doctor replied. "To the hospital!" she said, even more severely.

And so the informer had to go for shots by appointment. He was in quite a fix—the dog got him in the rear, and the doctors got him in the stomach.

And then somehow he got together with that "Soviet woman"—I don't know how. Maybe they had known each other before, but they ran into each other on the street. People like that recognize each other as do fishermen, fools, and informers. Birds of a feather . . . And they started talking. He told her he was limping because of being bitten by a dog with one black ear.

"I know him! I swear, I do!" the woman said. "He bit me, too."

Gray Man knew that she was lying, but he said, "I wrote a personal complaint and request to have it caught and put away. That's what my conscience told me to do."

"And rightly so!" the woman agreed heartily.

"You should write, too—if, of course, you're an honest person."

"Me? Of course I will!"

And that very day she brought her complaint over to the same veterinary station. In his heart of hearts, Gray Man was thinking, If you're going to lie to me, then let the doctors give *you* shots in the stomach. He didn't like being lied to, and he was proud of it. And she got into the same fix. She screamed and yelled and lied as best she could, saying the wound had been tiny and had already healed, pointing at an old scar on her hand, and shouting that she had written the complaint because she was an honest Soviet woman worried about the welfare of society and they were punishing her with shots in the stomach.

Strangely, they let her go for some reason, taking down her address and saying they would come to her house the next day to clear things up. So the woman hated Beem more than ever, and Gray Man, too, but not as much, even though he was the one who had sent her on the wild-goose chase.

Unhappily, as a result of the two complaints, the local paper carried this announcement:

There is reason to suspect that a half-breed setter with a black ear is biting pedestrians. Anyone knowing the whereabouts of the dog and any victims should contact the following address so that the dog can be examined and so that there will be no complications after any bites. Citizens! Protect your health and the health of others—don't keep quiet!

Letters from readers poured in. One of them said: "A dog was running toward the railroad station (a nonpedigreed setter, with a black ear). Without looking or listening, it just ran ahead. Well, dogs never run like that—straight across a square. This dog's tail was down, and its head was definitely lowered. The above-described dog (a setter with a black ear) is thoroughly dangerous, capable of biting any citizen of the Soviet Union or even a foreign tourist, and thus it must be caught and destroyed without any of the tests mentioned in the notice in your paper, which we admire."

There were twelve signatures at the bottom of this petition.

There were other letters (I can't list them all). Well, for instance, this one: "A dog exactly like that, but without the black ear, ran straight like that." Or: "The city is stuffed with dogs, and it's impossible to tell which are rabid." Or: "There's nothing wrong with that dog, you're the ones that are mad, you vets." Or: "If the regional executive committee can't organize a large-scale plan for years ahead to destroy dogs, then where are we headed, comrade editor? Where is the plan? Where is effective criticism, and why aren't you paying attention to it? We know how to bake bread, but we can't protect the health of the hardworking citizen. I'm an

97

honest man, and I always call a spade a spade. And I'm not afraid of anyone, by the way. You think about what I've said. I'm getting tired of waiting. I write and write, and nothing happens."

As I already said, there were too many letters to enumerate, but one must be cited. It had only two lines. A reader asked: "What if both ears are black—should I hit it, anyway?" That was a practical reader, far removed from an abstract perception of the world.

Finally the editor decided that the dog scandal was running wild and that it had apparently been created by the bitten man. And he acted wisely; he ran a notice in nonpareil type (which is never missed by the avid reader): "The dog with the black ear has been caught. The editors are closing all discussion on the topic. Manuscripts will not be returned."

But it wasn't true; Beem hadn't been caught. Tolik found out about the notice at school and went to the vet's apartment that evening, rang the doorbell, and, when the door opened, said,

"I'm here from Black Ear, from Beem."

The situation was cleared up quickly. The next day, Tolik picked up Beem and brought him to see the vet at the station. The doctor examined him and said, "This whole business is nonsense. The dog doesn't have rabies, it's just sick. It's been beaten and mutilated. People!" He sighed vaguely.

But he examined the sick paw, listened to Beem's insides, prescribed an ointment for the foot, gave him some medicine for his insides, and, as he saw the two friends out—the boy and the dog—he said, "What's your name, hero?"

"Tolik."

"You're a good fellow, Tolik. Bravo!"

Beem also thanked the doctor as they left. The man smelled of medicines, but he wasn't sick at all; on the contrary, he was tall and manly and had kind eyes.

"A good person," Beem said to him with his tail and his eyes. "You're a very good person."

Reader and friend! Not the reader who thinks that without his slanderous letters dogs will eat up all the citizens in the land. I mean you, my reader. Forgive me for inserting one or two satirical scenes in this story about a dog. Don't accuse me of breaking the laws of creativity, for each writer has his own laws. Don't accuse me of mixing genres, either, since life itself is a mixture. Good and evil, happiness and unhappiness, laughter and sorrow, truth and falsehood live side by side, and so close that it's difficult to tell them apart. I would feel worse if you found a half-truth in my story. It's like a half-empty barrel.

Most important, I believe in writing about everything. Just think! If you write about good only, that gives evil a field day; if you write about happiness only, then people will stop seeing unhappy folk and will finally stop noticing them; if you write only about the serious and the beautiful, then people will stop laughing at the ridiculous and ugly.

But I must admit that I'm writing only about a dog.

10

FOR MONEY

Thanks to the efforts of Tolik and Stepanovna, Beem started getting better. And in another two weeks, his foot began healing, though it remained splayed, broader than the others; he even tried stepping on it, but just a little—just a trial run. Beem's coat, brushed to a gloss by Tolik, enhanced his appearance. But his head ached constantly. The Gray Man's blows must have jarred something in it. Once in a while, he got dizzy; he would stop, wait in amazement to see what would happen to him, and then, thank God, it would stop until the next time. Sometimes a man traumatized or overwhelmed by an injustice will get a buzzing in his ears and feel dizzy and his heart will jump—and not necessarily right after the trauma, either. Then he'll stop with a lurch and wait in bitter surprise to see what will happen to him; and then the sensation really will go away, sometimes forever.

It was only in late fall, when the temperature had dropped steadily, that Beem began walking on all four feet. He still limped—the leg was shorter now. Yes, Beem was permanently crippled, but the problem with his head seemed to have passed. Truly, anything can happen and everything will pass.

Things would have been fine except for the fact that his master was still gone. And the sheet of paper didn't smell of him anymore and just lay in the corner like any other useless piece of paper. Beem could have gone on looking now, but Tolik never let him off the leash when they went out. Tolik was still worried by the notice in the paper, and he was afraid of the Gray Man. Sometimes people in the street would ask, "Isn't that the dog, the mad one, with a black ear?" Tolik would not reply but move away quickly, looking back. He could have said, "No, it's not," and put an end to it. But he didn't know how to lie or cover up feelings like fear, anxiety, or doubt; on the contrary, they were clearly written all over his face. He called a lie a lie, and the truth the truth. On top of that, he was developing a sense of humor, real humor, when something funny is said without a trace of a smile, and the speaker may be crying inside. The first manifestation of that humor had been his composition, which he himself didn't understand. He didn't understand anything completely; he was only beginning to guess certain things vaguely.

So, the boy in warm play pants and yellow shoes, a light-brown jacket, and a warm knit cap walked a lame dog down the same route every evening. He was always so neat and clean that anyone who saw him always thought, You can always tell, the boy is from a cultured family. People on the route were used to seeing him, and some even asked each other, "Who are the parents of that nice quiet boy?"

Tolik had become good friends with Stepanovna's granddaughter, a fair-skinned and fair-haired girl his age named Lusya, but he was too embarrassed to take her along on his walks with Beem. Once in a while, they played in the apartment with Beem, who repaid them with loyal love and constant attention, and Stepanovna brought her knitting so that she could enjoy the children at play.

Once, when they were combing out the long hair on Beem's legs and tail, Lusya asked Tolik, "Does your papa live here in town?"

"Yes. But they drive him to work in the morning and bring

him home late at night. He gets so tired! He says his nerves are pulled as tight as they'll go."

"And your mama?"

"Mama never has time. Never. It's either the washerwoman, or the floor cleaners, or her seamstress, or the phone constantly ringing—she never has a moment's peace. She can't even get away to come to parents' day at school."

"That's awful." Lusya sighed sincerely. She had only asked because she was always thinking about her parents. And so she said, "My mama and papa are far away. They went away by plane. Granny and I live alone." And she added merrily, not realizing how little it was, "We live on two rubles a day; that's how much we have!"

"It's enough, thank God," Stepanovna said. "You can buy ten loaves of white bread with it. That's plenty! But I remember what it was like a long time ago. That was terrible! I had to trade my husband's boots—that was your grandfather, Lusya—for a loaf of bread."

"When was that?" Tolik asked, raising his eyebrows.

"During the Civil War. A long time ago. You weren't even born yet. God spare you anything like that."

Tolik looked at Lusya and Stepanovna in amazement. He couldn't imagine that parents didn't live with their children or that once upon a time people paid for bread with boots.

Stepanovna guessed what he was thinking. "We can't leave, because we have to hold onto the apartment—we have to protect it or they'll take it away. And now I have to guard this one, too, until Ivan Ivanovich returns. Naturally! We're Ivan Ivanovich's neighbors, after all! And we don't want the apartments tooken!"

Beem looked at Stepanovna and figured it out: Ivan Ivanovich was alive! But where? He had to seek. And he begged to be let out. His wish was not granted. He lay down by the door and waited. Evidently he didn't need anyone else. Waiting!—

102

that was the goal of his life. To seek and to wait.

Tolik had caught Stepanovna's mistake in grammar, but he didn't correct it, the way he had the first time, because he respected the old lady, even though he wouldn't have been able to explain why—she was just Lusya's nice grandma. Beem loved Stepanovna, too. Tolik asked Beem, "Beem, do you love Stepanovna?"

Beem knew them all by name, he knew that there didn't exist a creature, not the lowliest dog, that didn't have a name, and he also knew whose slippers to bring when the children asked him to. And now, from Tolik and Stepanovna's eyes and her smile, Beem could tell that they were talking about her, and so he came over and put his head on her lap.

Before, Stepanovna had been indifferent to dogs ("Dogs are fine, but I have work to do"), but Beem had made her love him with his kindness, trust, and faithfulness to his master and friend.

The four creatures—three humans and one dog—were cozy and sweet in that strange apartment. Stepanovna felt warm and content. What else could you ask for in your old age?

Later, much later, many years later, Tolik will remember those late afternoons with the pale-violet window. He will. Of course, only if his heart stays open to people and if the leech of distrust doesn't attach itself to his heart. But on that evening he jumped up.

"I have to be home by nine. In bed at nine sharp. I'll bring you a drawing tablet and some Czech color pencils tomorrow, Lusya. You can't get pencils like that in a store for money or boots. They're imported!"

"Really?"

"Have you told your father where you spend your evenings?" Stepanovna asked.

"No-o. Why?"

"You have to tell him, Tolik. You must."

103

"He hasn't asked. And Mama hasn't. I'm always home by nine."

When Tolik was leaving, Beem begged persistently to be let out, but in vain. They were protecting him and taking care of him, but they didn't understand that he was pining for his friend, even though he loved them, too.

Tolik didn't come the next day. Lusya had been waiting eagerly for him to come with the sketchbook and pencils that you can't find in stores or buy for money. She waited so eagerly! She kept telling Beem, "Tolik's not here. Tolik's not coming."

Beem felt her anxiety, and it was long past Tolik's usual time, so the two of them kept looking out the window, waiting impatiently. But Tolik didn't appear.

He told his father, Stepanovna thought, and said aloud, "And we still have the dog. How will we manage without Tolik? Who'll take Beem out?"

Lusya's heart contracted, fearing something bad.

"I don't know," she said in a trembling voice.

Beem came over to her, looking at the small hands covering her face, and whimpered ("Don't be upset Lusya, don't"). He remembered how sometimes Ivan Ivanovich would sit at his desk and cover his face like that. That was bad—Beem knew that. Beem would always come over to him, and his master would pat his head and say, "Thanks, Beem, thanks." And Lusya lifted her face and patted Beem on the head.

"There, there, Lusya, that's all. Don't cry. Tolik will come. He will, don't worry, child. Tolik will come," her grandmother consoled her.

Beem limped to the door, trying to say, "Tolik will come. Let's go look for him."

"He wants to go out," Stepanovna said. "I'm beginning to understand him. We can't keep him in, he's a living creature."

Lusya stuck out her chin and said firmly, not quite herself, "I'll take him alone."

Stepanovna noticed how quickly the girl was growing up. And she was sad, too, that Tolik hadn't come.

A girl and a dog on the street. Three boys were coming toward them.

"Hey, girlie," the freckled redhead teased, "is that a boy dog or a girl dog you've got there?"

The three surrounded Lusya and Beem, and she was about to burst into tears, hurt by the teasing. But seeing that Beem's fur was bristling and that his head was lowered, she grew bold and shouted, "Get away from me!"

Beem barked so loud and strained toward them so wildly that the three scattered. Freckles, embarrassed by his hasty retreat, shouted from a distance, "Yah, yah! A girl with a big stud dog! Yah, yah! You should be ashamed!"

Lusya ran home as fast as her legs would carry her. Beem ran after. It was the first time in his life that he had encountered a bad child.

After that incident, they began letting Beem go out on his own. At first Lusya would go out with him and watch from the corner, whistling to keep him from straying too far. Then, one early morning, Stepanovna let him out alone. From that time on, he went out on his own, coming home in the evening and eating heartily.

But it had to happen! Once at an intersection, just as he was crossing a trolley line, someone called to him, "Beem!"

He looked up. A familiar conductor was leaning out of the trolley.

"Hey, Beem! Hello!"

Beem ran over and shook hands. It was the kind woman who used to take Beem and his master as far as the bus station when they were going hunting. Her!

"Where has your master been? Is Ivan Ivanovich sick?"

Beem shuddered: She knows, maybe she's on her way to see him now!

When the trolley started up, he jumped in. A woman passenger screamed and a man shouted, "Get out of here!" Some laughed, siding with Beem. The conductor stopped the trolley, calmed down the passengers (Beem noticed that), and said, "Go away, Beem. No. You can't ride without your master." She gave him a little shove. "No. Without Ivan Ivanovich, no."

What can you do? No means no. Beem sat and thought and then trotted off in the direction of the trolley. He had ridden along here with his master, he was sure—yes, there was the turn by the tower, and there was the traffic cop.

Beem ran along the trolley tracks, without crossing them even at the turns. A policeman whistled. Beem looked back without stopping and went on. He respected policemen; people like that never hurt him. He remembered his first time in a police station, he remembered everything, he was a smart dog; they left the station, Beem and Dasha, and went home, and everything was all right. And he had seen a policeman with a dog many times—a black one, very serious-looking at first. He made friends with it on the sidewalk one day; Ivan Ivanovich and the policeman let them talk to each other.

"He smells of the forest," the black dog said, looking up at the policeman.

"We went hunting yesterday," Ivan Ivanovich said.

"You're so clean!" Beem said, sniffing the dog.

"Of course! It's my job!" the black dog replied, wagging her tail.

To seal their budding friendship, both dogs signed the same tree, on the bottom.

No, the policeman was a good man, he liked dogs, you couldn't fool Beem on that.

He ran along the trolley tracks, off to one side, remembering that you can't step on the metal lines because they'll squash your foot.

At the end of the line, he followed the trolley's turnaround

106

circle and ended up at the stop. He sat and watched; the people here were all nice. So, that was a good start. Ivan Ivanovich and he used to cross the street here—over to the spot with the sign on the pole. Beem strolled over there and sat down with the small line of people waiting for the bus. He looked closely; there were no bad people here, either.

When the bus came, the line crawled into the door, and Beem went last, as befits a modest dog.

"Where do you think you're going?" the driver shouted. He took another look at Beem. "Wait a bit, just wait. I know you."

Beem knew that he was that friend who took the paper from his master's hand. And he wagged his tail.

"He remembers, the good dog!" the driver exclaimed. He thought a bit and then called Beem into the cab of the bus, "Come here!"

Beem sat down, close to the wall, to keep out of the way. He was agitated—this was the very driver who had taken them to the forest once, to hunt.

The bus roared and moved on. It grew silent at the stop where Ivan Ivanovich and Beem always got out. Beem lit up. He scratched at the door to the driver's cab, whined, begged, "Let me out. This is my stop."

"Sit!" the driver shouted.

Beem obeyed. The bus roared off. One of the passengers approached the driver and asked, "Is that your dog?"

"Yes."

"Is it trained?"

"Not very—but it's smart. See? Watch. Lie down!"

Beem lay down.

"Will you sell the dog? Mine died, and I have a flock of sheep to herd."

"All right."

"How much?"

"Twenty-five."

"Oh, boy!" the passenger said and left, first scratching Beem's ear. "Good dog, good dog."

Those kind words were very familiar to Beem; his master used them. And he wagged his tail at the stranger.

Beem no longer knew where he was going. But he watched through the windshield and noted the way, as dogs do when they go somewhere for the first time; that's how dogs are—they never forget the way back. Over the centuries people have lost that instinct almost completely. Too bad. It's important not to forget the way back.

At one of the stops the Good Man, who smelled of grass, got out. The driver did, too, leaving Beem in the cab. Beem watched intently. The driver pointed in Beem's direction; then he took the Good Man by the shoulder, and the man, smiling, took out papers and gave them to the driver. Then he adjusted his backpack, got into the cab, took off his belt, and attached it to Beem's collar.

"Let's go," he said. A few steps from the bus, he asked, "What's his name?"

The driver looked questioningly at Beem, then at his customer, and replied confidently, "Black Ear."

"It's not your dog, is it? Tell the truth."

"It's mine, it is. Black Ear. Really." And he drove off.

And so Beem was sold for money.

He knew that something wrong was going on. But the man who smelled of grass was obviously good, and Beem went along with him, sad and upset.

They walked in silence, and suddenly the man addressed Beem, "No, Black Ear isn't your name. People don't call their dogs that. And when your master shows up, he'll give me my twenty-five rubles. That goes without saying."

Beem watched him, head cocked, as if to say, "I don't understand you."

"I can see that you're a smart dog, a good one."

108

There were those words again, so often spoken by his master. Beem wagged his tail to show gratitude for the kindness.

"Well, if that's the case, then live with me," the man said.

And they went on. Twice, Beem tried to hold back, pulling on the leash and looking over his shoulder ("Let me go, I'm not going your way").

The man stopped, stroked the dog, and said, "Never mind . . . never mind . . ."

It would have been easy enough—just tug at the belt once or twice and chew it through. But Beem knew that a leash was to lead a dog and to keep it from going too far. And he stopped begging.

They walked through a forest. The trees were thoughtful and silent—naked, cold, calmed by the frost. The grass in the forest was limp, faded, and tangled—dreary. Beem felt desolate.

Then they crossed a field of winter wheat, soft and cheery. Beem felt better here; there was lots of room and lots of sky, and the man next to him was whistling—he always felt good when Ivan Ivanovich did that. But when their path reached the plowed fields, he felt depressed again. The dark-gray soil was flecked with chalk, and there were no lumps. It seemed lifeless —just dusty, worn-out soil.

The man stepped off the road, dug his heel in the soil, and sighed.

"It's bad, brother," he said to Beem. "A couple more black storms and the soil will be done for. It's bad, brother."

Beem knew the words "bad, brother" from Ivan Ivanovich, and he knew that they meant sadness, depression, or that something "wasn't right," and he took the words "black storm" to be a variation on "black ear" that he didn't understand. But Beem couldn't understand anything about soil. The man realized this.

"But you're a dog, and you don't understand. But who can I talk to? So I'm complaining to you, Blackie. Wait a minute!" He looked at Beem and said, "That's what I'll call you. Blackie.

109

That's a good name for a dog. After your black ear."

By the time they reached the village, Beem knew that now his name was Blackie. The man had repeated it gently many times: "Blackie, that's good." Or he'd say, "Good boy, Blackie, you're walking fine." Whatever he said, he always added "Blackie."

And so people sold Beem's good name for money. Luckily, Beem didn't know that, as he didn't know that other people would sell their honor, loyalty, and hearts for those pieces of paper.

And now Beem had to forget his name. What could he do—it was his fate. But he wouldn't forget his friend, Ivan Ivanovich. He was beginning a new life, completely different from anything he had known, but he wouldn't forget *him*.

11

BLACKIE IN THE COUNTRY

The village he was brought to amazed Beem. People lived here, too, but everything was different from where he had been born and raised. The houses were small—and stood right on the ground, without stairs or landings, without lots of doorways, and the doors didn't have clicking locks. At night, they were locked with bolts from the inside. In the morning, at the same time, smoke rose from the roof of every house, but the houses didn't go anywhere, they just stood in even rows and smoked silently, without a rumble.

The most amazing thing for Beem (or Blackie) was that various animals and birds lived along with the people—cows, chickens, sheep, pigs—and it took awhile to become acquainted with them. Behind the people's houses, the animals had their own houses, covered with straw or reeds and fenced in by plaited sticks and twigs. And no one bothered anyone—the people didn't harm the animals and birds, the animals didn't attack the people, and no one used a gun.

On the first day, Beem was given a bed of fresh straw in the corner of the porch. The man tied him with a stout rope, fed him well, and went off somewhere in a raincoat. Beem spent the rest of the day alone in total silence. At evening he heard hoofbeats as the sheep came into the yard, and he heard the cow mooing in the shed (she was asking for something). And soon the man was back, with a boy in a raincoat and boots and hat, carrying a long stick. His face was as brown as the man's, and he smelled of sheep.

"Well, Alyosha, meet your new comrade."

They approached Beem.

"Papa, he won't bite, will he?"

"No, Alyosha, dogs like this don't bite. Hello, Blackie. Blackie is a good dog." And he slapped him lightly on the side.

Beem lay still and watched the boy. He stroked Beem, too.

"Blackie, Blackie . . ." And he turned to the grown-up. "Papa, if we untie him, will he run away?"

"Let's wait a bit." He went inside the house.

Beem stood up and then sat down and offered his paw to the boy, as if to say, "Hello. You're a good person."

"Papa!" the boy shouted. "Papa, come here!"

He returned.

"Hello, Blackie!" The boy gave him his hand.

Beem shook once more. Both people were obviously pleased by his politeness. Those first minutes of getting to know them were important ones for Beem. He learned that the man who had brought him here was called Papa and the boy was Alyosha. Even common ordinary strays soon learn people's names, but Beem—why go on?

Then, after dark, a woman came home, too. She was dressed strangely; she had two scarves on her head, and her padded jacket fit tight as a drum, and her padded pants were just like the ones worn by the Good Woman who drove spikes on the railroad. But she smelled of earth and beets (a sweet root that Beem never said no to). She went into the house, talked to the men about something, and then went out through the porch carrying a bucket. Now, without moving, Beem had learned that the porch had one door leading to the street, one to the animals, and a third into the house. But the rope didn't let him reach any of them. That was all he had learned so far.

He lay down again.

There was a very strong sheep smell coming from the yard. Beem had learned what sheep were a long time ago. He had thought that they lived in flocks and walked around meadows and didn't do anything except eat and bleat. And there was always a man near them, a man in a waterproof cape carrying a long crook; such a man had approached Beem and Ivan Ivanovich once, when they were resting by a haystack, and had shaken hands with Beem's master. A big shaggy dog was with him. Beem made friends with it in an unusual way. Fuzzy ran at him barking loudly, but Beem rolled over on his back with his legs in the air, and said, "What's the matter? Have I done something to offend you?"

Politeness won out over rudeness, of course, and Fuzzy sniffed Beem and licked his stomach and then walked away a bit and signed a rock. Beem followed suit. That meant that peace had been made. And while Beem's master talked to Fuzzy's, they played tag, and Beem turned out to be much faster and nimbler, earning Fuzzy's undisguised admiration. When they parted (they had to follow their masters, after all!), they sniffed the rock and exchanged a look.

"Come by sometime," Beem said and bounded away.

"There's so much work," Fuzzy said and made his way back to the herd, lowering his head.

That was in the past. And now the smell of sheep again. When he smelled them, in a strange house, in the fading light, alone, without people, feeling so low, Beem couldn't help remembering Ivan Ivanovich.

Then he heard a rhythmic pattern of liquid hitting metal: *psssst! pssssst!* Beem didn't know what it was. The unfamiliar noise stopped, and the woman came in from the yard, still carrying the bucket. And it smelled of milk. What a smell! Beem had never smelled milk like that in town. This was very different, but milk nevertheless. In the city, milk didn't smell of

113

human hands, or various pleasant herbs, or of cows, that's for sure. Here it all blended into a wonderful aroma, deliciously pink and warm. Let's not argue the point; if even a human being can sometimes distinguish real milk from store milk, then how could Beem, with his acute sense of smell, miss that astounding blend of hands and flowers and grass. And so he jumped up quickly and wagged his tail at the woman. But she probably couldn't understand his joy.

In the four long years of his life, he had never seen a cow milked. And milk smelled of cows. So the confusion remained —there were things he didn't know. But there are so many things a dog doesn't know. And if some dog says that he knows everything and is sure that he can teach you what to do and how to do it and where, well, even a chicken won't believe him; it doesn't matter that he's stronger than a chicken—it won't believe him. Take the Scottish terrier, for instance; he pretends that his blockhead is stuffed with ideas (he's got a beard, a mustache, and eyebrows—a real philosopher!), when he's really silly, bossy, grumbles at his master day and night like a neurotic, and is always up to no good. And he can't do anything. Not a bit! He gets by on his looks. Inside, it's all fluff or empty space.

But Beem was something else; he was sincere and honest. If he didn't know something, he was the first to say so: "I don't know that." If he didn't like someone, he would say, "You are a bad person. Go away! Woof!" And he would bark enough to scare the daylights out of anybody.

He felt deep respect for the woman who got that divine milk from somewhere. And he kept looking at the door she had passed through with the milk.

Someone came up from the street and opened the door.

"Who is it?" Beem demanded. "Woof!"

The Visitor reeled back. Papa ran out of the house, turned on the porch light, and asked, "Who's there?"

"It's me, the brigade leader."

114

And the Visitor came back on the porch and shook hands (so, they were friends—that meant no more barking), and approached Beem.

Papa crouched, petted Beem, and said, "You're a good boy, Blackie. Good boy, you know your job." He untied him and led him inside.

The most important thing was that there was a lame chicken in the room. Beem looked at it and pointed, raising his front foot, but uncertainly, as if to say, "What kind of bird is that? I've never encountered one—"

"Look!" Papa exclaimed. "What a wonderful dog, that Blackie, he's a jack of all trades!"

But since the chicken paid absolutely no mind to Beem's point, he sat down, still giving it a sidelong glance or two, which in dog language meant: "What else! That's all I need! Just try something." And then he looked at the people.

"And he won't harm chickens!" Alyosha cried.

Beem watched his face carefully.

"And his eyes! Mama, look at his eyes! They're human," Alyosha went on. "Blackie, come here, come to me!"

Wouldn't Beem respond to sheer joy? Of course he went and sat beside Aloysha.

There was conversation around the table. Papa uncorked a bottle; Mama served food. The brigade leader emptied his glass. So did Papa. So did Mama. Alyosha didn't drink for some reason, but ate ham and bread. He threw a piece of bread in the middle of the room, but Beem didn't budge (you had to say "take it").

"Indeed he is intelligent," the brigade leader, his face glowing, said. "He doesn't eat bread."

The chicken limped over and dragged away the piece meant for Beem. They all laughed, but Beem looked attentively at Alyosha; it was no laughing matter if there was no mutual understanding in a friendly atmosphere.

"Wait a minute, Alyosha," Papa said. He put another piece of

115

bread on the floor, chased the chicken away, and spoke directly to Beem: "Take it, Blackie. Take it!"

Beem swallowed the tasty morsel with pleasure, even though he was full.

The brigade leader put a piece of ham on the floor.

"No!" he warned.

Beem sat still. The chicken was sidling over to the ham, but just as it was about to grab it, Beem snorted at it, almost pushing it with his nose. The chicken scurried under the bed.

"Blackie, take it!" the brigade leader said.

Beem politely ate that morsel as well.

"That's it!" shouted Papa. He was always loud and kind, but when he got red he was even kinder. "Blackie is an extraordinary marvel!" And he hugged him.

They're good people, Beem thought. He really liked Papa's mustache, soft and furry, which he felt when Papa hugged him.

And then a conversation ensued, of which Beem understood only the word "sheep," but he was sure that the two men were arguing.

"Look, Khrisan Andreyevich, let's get down to business," the brigade leader said, putting his hand on Papa's shoulder. "Do sheep want to eat or not?"

"They do," Papa answered. "But my turn is over. My turn was until the Feast of Intercession, and it's come and gone."

"The sheep are personal property, not kolkhoz property, and they're hungry. The kolkhoz members are driving me crazy. There's no snow, there's plenty of feed underfoot, the sheep should graze until the snows come. And they're right."

" 'Until the snows.' So they think I'm made of steel? And Alyosha?"

"Until the snows, Khrisan Andreyevich," the brigade leader insisted. "We'll pay you double. All right?"

"No. My woman is killing herself over the beets; we have to help her, and you keep harping on the snows."

116

But then they slapped each other's hands in agreement and stopped talking about the sheep and the snows. And the three of them walked the brigade leader to the door, forgetting about Beem.

He went out on the porch, too, then ran around the yard, stood at the fence, sniffing the sheep smells, which reminded him of his favorite human, his one and only, and then he sat down undecidedly.

It was night. An autumn night in the country, quiet, hiding from the winter, but ready to greet it. Everything in that night was strange for Beem. Dogs generally don't like traveling at night (except for strays who have lost their faith in man and try to avoid him), and Beem— Well, it goes without saying! Beem was in doubt for now. And Alyosha was such a nice boy.

Alyosha's voice interrupted his doubts. He was calling anxiously, "Bla-ackie!"

Beem ran up and went into the porch with him. Alyosha put him down, added more hay to his bedding, caressed him, and went off to bed.

It grew quiet. There were no trolleys, no buses, no car horns —nothing familiar.

A new life had begun.

Beem had learned that Papa was also Khrisan Andreyevich, and also Father, and that Mama was also Petrovna, and that Alyosha was Alyosha. And he didn't exactly despise the chicken, but he didn't respect it, either. As far as dogs were concerned, birds absolutely had to fly, and this one only walked, and therefore wasn't worthy of respect, since it was wingless and defective to boot. And then there were the sheep. They reminded him of Ivan Ivanovich; Alyosha smelled of them, too. Petrovna smelled of earth and beets. And earthy smells always excited Beem. Perhaps Ivan Ivanovich would come here, too. . . .

Beem fell asleep, warm and cozy in the aromatic hay. Lying in hay like that, even a man will fall asleep immediately, and the

117

smell of fresh hay evokes a blue color in front of his eyes just before sleep comes. Beem had a more acute sense of smell than any man, and every nuance of the aroma soothed him and softened his pain.

Beem was awakened by a rooster crowing. He had heard roosters before, but never this close—this one was right on the other side of the wall, screaming, "Cock-a-doodle-doo!" proudly and loudly. All the roosters of the village responded. (A little later, Beem would learn that this rooster was the leader and that such birds are usually quite mean.) Beem sat and listened to the amazing music; it rolled across the village in waves, sometimes closer, sometimes farther away, depending on which rooster's turn it was, and the last one crowed a pathetic little cock-a-doodle-doo, hoarsely and not at all like a rooster worthy of respect. Later, with time, Beem would learn that that rooster was a coward and would run even from a strange rooster that burst into his chicken yard, even though the coward was supposed to defend the peace and quiet of the hens in his domain. And yet it's precisely that kind of rooster that is merciless with strange chicks—he pecks them, the louse, even though any self-respecting rooster would never peck a chick that had wandered in by mistake. So that rooster crows last, and only when he is sure that it is the right time. And Beem had no idea, through lack of experience, that no one ever tells time by such lousy half-roosters.

Beem lay down to nap. Then the singing rolled from one end of the village to the other once more. And Beem sat up and listened to it with great pleasure. And then, a third time, even stronger and fuller and, really, more exalted. Ah, they sing beautifully! That was marvelous! And what they were doing way off in the distance, you couldn't even imagine! Beem still didn't know that the beautiful crowing was coming from the kolkhoz poultry farm, where the gorgeous snow-white, confident roosters were singing. If he hadn't been locked up in the porch, Beem would have run over to the farm to see and hear the marvel close up. But the porch was his cage.

Slowly and gradually, the gray autumn dawn crept in through a crack in the door. Beem got up and examined the porch. There was a tub full of grain, a bin with corncobs in one corner, and one with cabbages in the other. That was it.

Petrovna came out with the bucket. Beem greeted her. She went out into the yard, and Beem followed her. She sat next to the cow. Beem sat nearby. Streams of milk rang in the bucket, and Beem moved his front paws in amazement. Milk! The cow stood there calmly and chewed her cud, and the milk seemed to come on its own—she was like a cozy live cistern with its taps open.

Petrovna finished milking, called Beem ("Blackie!"), poured some milk into a bowl, said "no," waited a bit, said "take," laughed kindly, and hurried back into the house.

Ah, what wonderful milk that was! Warm and aromatic. You could smell grass, and flowers, and fields—all together—and (now he was sure!) Petrovna's own hands, not just hands in general, as Beem had thought yesterday from a distance. Beem lapped it all up, licked the bowl, performed his morning ablutions, and quickly checked the yard. The cow accepted him with complete trust; even licking his head, which prompted Beem to put his tongue on her rough, milky nose. The sheep stamped their feet at him from the other side of the fence, but stopped when they saw that he had no aggressive intentions. The pig and her two piglets did not deign to recognize Beem that first time and just snorted ironically among themselves and didn't stir, even though they were lying with their heads toward Beem, by the fence. That was Beem's debut among the four-legged animals. But the chickens—that was something else! Actually, not the chickens, but the red rooster. As soon as he flew down from his perch, he flapped his wings and grumbled angrily, "Ko-ko-ko-ko!" And he attacked like a hawk. The red

119

rooster with the red comb hit the dog with his claws (that's the kind of rooster he was!). Beem barked and swiped at him with his paw. And the rooster lowered his wings and ran to the corner where the hens were gathered in a nervous rooting section; he ran from Beem in total ignominy but reached the hens a hero. He even called out, "See how I gave it to him! Like that and that!" The hens were obviously cheering the rooster with all their chicken strength. And Beem looked at the rooster with respect. Say what you will, but Beem had never seen a bird attack a dog so bravely. And that meant something, after all.

"What's all this ruckus?" Khrisan Andreyevich asked as he came out into the yard. "Shush, you!" he yelled at the chickens. "Scared of the dog, are you?" He pulled Beem over to the chickens by the collar and stood there with him for a while.

Beem walked away and turned his back on them—the heck with them! From that moment on, the chickens and rooster left Beem alone, but they didn't seem particularly afraid of him, either. One would cackle at him and then jump out of his path. What did he care? Chickens walked and didn't fly or swim, and no one shot at them. That meant they weren't birds but just some ridiculous creatures. The rooster was a different story. He flew up on the roof and could warn of a stranger's approach almost faster than Beem, and he ruled with dignity—he wouldn't eat a worm alone, but would call his subjects and divide up the worm for them. The rooster was quite worthy of his title.

Since Beem was not allowed out of the yard for the first week, he became boss there; he would lie in the center and watch with his eyes. He knew all the chickens by the fourth day, and when a strange chicken flew over the fence, he let her have it so hard that she cackled for a long time after, running off and then coming back and hopping in one spot and looking around in fear and curiosity.

A piglet offered his friendship very quickly; he went up to

Beem, snorted, prodded his neck lightly with his damp snout, and looked at him with his dumb, light-lashed eyes. Beam licked his snout. The piglet loved it and jumped up in pleasure and then stamped around Beem, his little feet raising the dust. Beem condescendingly moved to another spot, but the piglet followed him. It muttered something incomprehensible (pigs and dogs can't understand each other, like foreigners) and lay down, snuggling close to Beem's furry back. And so, on one cold day when Beem felt chilly and lonely (the door to the porch was shut during the day), no one from the yard was surprised to see Beem sleeping between the piglets on soft hay, warmed on both sides. The piglets' mother had no objections to this friendship; on the contrary, every time Beem came into their pen, she moaned with pleasure (not pain).

Beem was fed very well; and besides, the piglets, who were growing fast and were almost half Beem's size, didn't mind if he had a taste of their swill once in a while. Every morning he received a quart of milk, which was considered a trifle around here. You might ask: What more could a dog want? But the yard was a yard, a caged camp, fenced in with locked gates. This was not the life for a hunting dog—lying around, guarding hens, bringing up piglets—not at all, particularly for a dog as outstanding as Beem.

He had gotten used to the yard and its inhabitants and was no longer surprised by its abundance of food. But whenever the wind blew from the meadows, Beem paced restlessly from one wall of the fence to the other or stood on his hind legs against it, as though he wanted to get just a little closer to the heights, and looked up into the sky where doves flew, free and light. Something was nagging at him from within, and he guessed vaguely that even with all the food and the kind treatment, there was still something very important missing.

Ah, you flying doves, you don't know anything about well-fed dogs in captivity!

Beem also sensed that they didn't trust him, since they didn't let him out. Every morning Khrisan Andreyevich and Alyosha herded the sheep from the yard and led them away for the day, with their raincoats and crooks. And Beem, no matter how hard he begged, was always left in the yard.

One day Beem was lying in the yard, nose pressed against the fence, and the wind brought him the news—there's a meadow out there, and a forest nearby. Freedom was near! Through a crack in the fence, he saw a dog run by. And he couldn't stand it anymore. He clawed at the earth under the fence, clawed again, and then set to work. He dug the hole with his front paws and moved it under him, and threw it farther away with his hind legs. He could even use his hurt foot, but not as efficiently.

I don't know what would have happened then, but just as Beem was finishing his tunnel, the sheep came into the yard. They saw the earth flying from the fence and reared back at the gate where Alyosha was. The sheep knocked him over and ran down the street, berserk. Alyosha ran after them, but Beem didn't pay any attention to anything. He went on digging.

Khrisan Andreyevich came over and held him by the tail. Beem froze in his tunnel, playing dead.

"Lonely, huh, Blackie?" Khrisan Andreyevich asked, lightly tugging on Beem's tail, inviting him back in.

Beem crawled out. What can you do if they pull you by the tail?

"What's the matter, Blackie?" Khrisan Andreyevich let go and backed off. "You haven't got rabies, do you?"

Beem's eyes were bloodshot; he was twitching nervously, panting, moving his nose from side to side, as though he had just finished an exhausting, tense hunt. He ran around the yard in agitation and finally began scratching at the gate, looking back at Khrisan Andreyevich.

The man stood in the middle of the yard in deep thought. Beem came up to him, sat, and said clearly with his eyes, "I have to get out there, to be free. Let me out, let me!" He groveled on his stomach and whimpered so pathetically and softly that Khrisan Andreyevich bent down and stroked him.

"Oh, Blackie, Blackie . . . Dogs want to be free, too. Life is hard!" He called Beem into the porch, put him down on the hay, tied him with a rope, and brought him a bowl of meat.

That was it. A well-fed life without freedom disgusted Beem. He didn't touch the meat.

12

IN THE FREEDOM OF THE FIELDS, AN UNUSUAL HUNT, AND FLIGHT

In the morning, everything followed the usual routine: the spring of the working day began unwinding with the roosters' third crow, the cow mooed, Petrovna milked her and then lit the stove, Alyosha came out to play with his beloved Blackie, Papa fed the cow, the pigs, and the chickens, and then they sat down to breakfast. Beem didn't touch the aromatic milk, even though Alyosha begged and cajoled him. Then, while his parents were busy with their household chores, Alyosha brought water and cleaned out the cow's stall and begged Beem to eat again, shoving his nose in the bowl, but alas, Blackie acted almost like a stranger. When Khrisan Andreyevich was ready to leave for work, he sharpened a huge knife and stuck it over the door.

As the sun came up, Petrovna wrapped herself up in her heavy clothes and shawls, took her bag and the huge knife that Papa had sharpened, and left. Alyosha and his father, dressed in their raincoats, went into the yard, and Beem could hear them driving the sheep into the street.

Could they really be leaving Beem alone and tied up in the dark porch? Beem couldn't stand it—he began howling bitterly and hopelessly.

And then the door from the street opened. Khrisan Andreyevich came in, untied Beem and led him out onto the stoop, and locked the door. He took him over to the flock of sheep, handed Alyosha the rope that was tied to Beem's collar, and went to the front of the flock.

"Let's go, let's go!" he shouted.

The sheep followed him down the street. Five or ten sheep from every house joined them, so that by the time they reached the outskirts of the village, he had a huge number of sheep. Khrisan Andreyevich was still in front, and Alyosha and the dog were in back.

The day was crisp and dry, and the dirt under their feet was almost as hard as the cement in the city, but less smooth. Snowflakes started dancing in the air, blocking the cold sun from view, but they soon stopped. It was no longer autumn but not yet winter, a wary interim period when winter was just around the corner, anticipated, but neverthelesslikelytoarriveunexpectedly.

The sheep trotted briskly and bleated in their drawling sheep language. Beem noticed that a big ram with curved horns walked directly behind Khrisan Andreyevich and that a small lame ewe straggled at the very back, just in front of Alyosha. Alyosha prodded her lightly with his crook to keep her from lagging behind, and called out, "Papa, slow down a bit! The lame one can't keep up!"

Papa slowed down without looking back, and the whole flock slowed down, too.

Beem was on the rope. He saw how important Papa was as he walked in front of the flock and how they all obeyed his slightest movement, and he saw how Alyosha watched the sheep, keeping them in line from the sides and from behind. One of them wandered off to pick at the stubbly yellow grass. Alyosha and Beem ran over.

"Where do you think you're going?" Alyosha threw his crook in front of her.

125

The sheep turned back. On the left, three sheep suddenly decided to show some independence, and headed for a green patch, but Alyosha ran after them and put them in their place. Beem very quickly learned that the sheep had to stay together, and the next time he and Alyosha ran after one, he barked at the sheep for disrupting the social order: "Woof-woof-woof!" There was no anger; it had the same meaning as Alyosha's "Where do you think you're going?"

"Papa! Do you hear?" Alyosha called.

Khrisan Andreyevich turned and yelled, "Good boy, Blackie!"

On the slope of the ravine, he raised his crook above his head and yelled just as loudly, "Let them go—oo-o!" And walking slowly, he cut back through the flock.

Alyosha began doing the same thing, but he moved quickly from the back, almost running, pressing the sheep toward Khrisan Andreyevich. And the flock began spreading out gradually, finally stretching out into a line no more than two or three deep, nibbling grass. Khrisan Andreyevich stopped, facing the sheep, and looked up and down the line. The chief ram stood next to him. The shepherd took a loaf of bread from his satchel, cut off a piece of crust, and gave it to the ram. Beem couldn't have known that not only must the chief ram not fear the shepherd; he must actually love him. As far as Beem was concerned, the action was only one more proof of Papa's kindness and generosity. But to tell the truth, Papa was a crafty man—the ram followed him around like a puppy and always came when called. Khrisan Andreyevich knew that a stupid ram in a small flock, especially one without a dog, could lead the sheep almost anywhere—just let the tired shepherd fall asleep in the hot sun and they'll be gone. So this ram was a specially trained one, and therefore he accepted Beem easily.

Khrisan Andreyevich lit his pipe and said to Alyosha, "Don't push, don't push it—this is good grazing right here."

126

It's not easy to feed sheep in late autumn; in unskilled hands, half the flock starves to death in a week, even though good grazing is available—they'll just trample it and waste it. But if the shepherd knows what he's doing, the sheep can fatten on average grazing. Khrisan Andreyevich managed to feed his flock on empty fields and forest edges, under the noses of tractors tearing up the ground—and you need a special talent and vocation and love of animals to be able to do that. It's tough work, herding sheep, and also beautiful work, because the shepherd, without thinking about it, feels that he is part of nature as well as its master and benefactor.

And so the sheep were nibbling and cropping the grass and chomping so merrily that the sound, calm, steady, and soothing, rose over the field. Papa and Alyosha were close to each other now and could talk in normal voices, without shouting.

Alyosha asked, "Papa, should I free Blackie?"

"Let's try. He oughtn't to run off now; dogs don't run for freedom. But wait and play with him a bit, and don't scare the sheep."

Alyosha waited for the flock to move away, untied Beem's rope, and called, "Blackie! Let's run!" And he ran down the hill toward the ravine, his boots striking the ground noisily.

Beem was ecstatic. He leaped in the air, trying to lick Alyosha's cheek on the run, ran off, and shot back like an arrow, enjoying his freedom; then he grabbed a stick and offered it to Alyosha. Alyosha took it, threw it quite a long way, and said, "Fetch, Blackie!"

Beem brought it back. Alyosha threw it again, but this time he didn't take it from Beem's mouth, but went up the hill, saying, "Blackie, hold it. Carry!"

Beem followed him with his burden. When they got to the top, Alyosha replaced the stick with his cap. Beem carried it with pleasure. Alyosha ran ahead, repeating, "Carry, Blackie. Carry, you good boy. That's good. Good dog."

127

But they approached the flock carefully ("Don't scare the sheep"). Alyosha ordered, "Give the cap to Papa."

Khrisan Andreyevich extended his hand. Beem gave him the cap. Beem's new ability came as a surprise to the shepherds. All three delighted in it.

And in less than a week, Beem had figured out for himself that he had a new responsibility: keeping headstrong sheep in the fold, watching them when they were let loose into the line, and letting them go into their own yards on their return trip through the village.

Beem made friends with the two dogs who guarded the huge kolkhoz flock, which needed three shepherds, all of them grown-ups and all wearing raincoats. Even though the kolkhoz and the private flocks never mixed, Alyosha would run over to see the shepherds when they stopped nearby, and Beem went with him to see the dogs. They were good dogs, pale yellow, hairy, and big, but very calm and docile; they even played with Beem in a calm, condescending way, and they walked around the flock instead of leaping and bounding the way Beem did; these were dogs with a great sense of dignity. Beem liked them. And the sheep were nice, too.

Beem began a free working life. They may have returned tired and therefore quiet, but they were free and worked in mutual trust. Dogs don't run from a life like that.

Suddenly it snowed, and the wind swirled, blowing hard. Khrisan Andreyevich, Alyosha, and Beem ran the sheep into a circle, stood around for a while, and finally drove the sheep back to the village in the middle of the day. There was white snow on the sheep, on the men's shoulders, on the ground. The white snow was everywhere—there was nothing but snow in the fields, nothing else. Winter had appeared; it just dropped out of nowhere.

Khrisan Andreyevich must have decided that a dog like Beem shouldn't be sleeping with the pigs or be tied up on the porch, and Beem was moved to a warm kennel built for him in the corner of the porch and packed with soft hay. In the evenings he came into the house like a member of the family and stayed there until after supper.

"It can't be winter yet. It's too early," Khrisan Andreyevich said to Petrovna.

They used the word "winter" a lot in conversation, worrying about something or other; Beem just knew that winter meant white, cold snow.

That evening, Petrovna came home powdered with snow, wet, her face frostbitten and swollen. Beem saw her shaking her hands and moaning. Her hands were cracked raw and covered with dark calluses almost like the pads on Beem's paws. She soaked her hands in warm water, washed them, and then spent a long time rubbing in salve and moaning. And Khrisan Andreyevich looked at Petrovna and seemed sad about something. (Beem could tell from his face.)

The next morning, he sharpened some knives, and all four of them went out—Petrovna, Khrisan Andreyevich, Alyosha, and Beem. They walked through a smooth white field covered by a light coat of snow—no more than half a paw deep, so it was easy going. It was quiet and cold. Then they reached a field with row upon row of beets in great heaps. Beside each heap sat a woman, dressed just like Petrovna, and they were all doing something in silence and with great concentration.

The four went up to a pile of beets, sat around it, and Beem watched carefully to see what would happen. Petrovna grabbed a top and pulled a beet from the pile, deftly turned the root toward her and—chop!—cut off the leaves with her knife. Two more slices on the root and it was clean. And she threw it down next to her. Khrisan Andreyevich duplicated her movements. And so did Alyosha, even more quickly than Papa. And the work was on! Chop! Away with the leaves. Chop-chop! The root was clean. Thud—and the roots were in a pile, a new, clean pile.

129

Not far away, a woman sat alone beside a similar pile and did the same thing. There were three people at the next one. The whole field was like that—piles of beets, bundled-up women with cracked hands and faces swollen from the cold. They worked in light tarpaulin gloves or barehanded. Chop-chop! No more leaves. Chop-chop! No more leaves. Chop-chop! And the person drops the knife and blows on her hands, rubs them together, and then, chop-chop! a clean root. And the hours pass that way. Like clockwork.

It was cold. Watching the knives, Beem began to shiver, so he got up and roamed around the vicinity. He warmed up and returned to his pile, even though other women had invited him to visit (everyone in the village knew Blackie).

Then the woman who had been working all alone came over. She was young but very thin. She complained about something, blowing her nose without a hankie, and then sat next to Petrovna and showed her her hands. Petrovna showed hers. The woman was sad, then coughed, clutching her mitten to her chest, and fell silent. Her name was Natalya.

Petrovna—chop-chop! Khrisan Andreyevich—chop-chop! Alyosha—chop-chop! And they blew on their fingers and rubbed their cheeks. Petrovna—chop-chop! And then—plop! A teardrop fell from the sad woman's eyes onto a leaf. She covered her face with her sleeve and went back to her pile.

"Heaven forbid, I don't want you catching cold," Petrovna said to Alyosha. She checked his warm scarf under his cap, tucked it in around his neck, and removed a canvas sash from her waist and wrapped it around the boy's sheepskin jacket.

Beem thrust his nose in Alyosha's jacket, helping Petrovna. But Beem found that Alyosha wasn't as cold as he seemed to be; in fact he was much warmer than Papa or Mama (Beem could judge that much better than people).

"Listen, Alyosha," Khrisan Andreyevich said, working for

130

two with his knife. (Beem perked up his ears.) "You go play with Blackie, warm up a bit."

And Beem ran ahead of the boy down the beet field, rock-hard from the frost. They crossed the field, and Alyosha got hot, so he removed the cap, untied the scarf, stuck it inside his jacket, and replaced his cap with the flaps up. Next to the forest strip, Beem stopped in the thick yellow grass, sniffed the air, made a cast, and froze like a statue, surprising Alyosha.

Alyosha ran up to him. "What is it, what's here, Blackie?"

Beem stood motionless and waited for the order. Alyosha figured out what was going on. "Scare them! Scare 'em!" he yelled.

Beem was waiting for the magic word "forward." But Alyosha shouted even louder, "Scare 'em!"

Beem moved in on them and flushed a covey of partridges. Alyosha hurried back with him to where his parents were working, and Beem realized they didn't understand each other again —Alyosha didn't know Ivan Ivanovich's words—but he ran alongside, anyway. And the boy, red and panting, told his parents how Blackie found the partridges and "scared" them.

"Blackie is a hunting dog; he's trained." Khrisan Andreyevich was impressed. "If we only had a gun, Alyosha! Then we could hunt. How about that?"

Gun? Hunt? What familiar and dear words for Beem! He knew what they meant.

Beem wagged his tail, nuzzled up to Alyosha, Khrisan Andreyevich, and Petrovna; he spoke to them in his language clearly and distinctly. But no one here understood him; no one went for the gun, and no one went hunting even without a gun. So Beem sat behind Alyosha, cuddling up to the sheepskin.

They got home at dusk, tired and chilled. A few days later, they stopped going to the fields—the work was done.

Now Petrovna didn't go out to work and was obviously pleased. She did something all day long: cleaned the cowshed, washed clothes, washed floors, chopped cabbage, churned but-

131

ter, kindled the stove, cooked, sewed, mended, fed the cow—
you couldn't list it all. Beem watched her work.

A clean woman carrying books came for Alyosha, scolding
Petrovna (but not angrily, Beem noted); both women said
"Alyosha," "sheep," and "beets." The next day, early in the
morning, Alyosha left with books under his arm, and disappeared every day after that. Khrisan Andreyevich went off
every day with a pitchfork, and when he came back in the
evenings he smelled of manure.

One evening, when they were all eating, a man came in. He
was tall, broad, and bony, with a large face and small, foxy eyes.
He was wearing a fox cap. Beem noticed that Khrisan Andreyevich didn't smile at the Visitor, or get up from the table
the way he usually did, or offer his hand.

"Hello," the Visitor said tonelessly, keeping his hat on.

"Hello, Klim," Khrisan Andreyevich replied. "Sit down."

He sat on a bench, rolled a huge cigarette for himself, looking
at Beem all the while, and said, "So this is Blackie." (Beem
perked up his ears.) "The dog is being wasted without hunting.
It'll run away. Sell it to me, I'll give you twenty-five."

"It's not for sale," Khrisan Andreyevich said, and rose from
the table, his supper over.

Beem could tell from three feet away—the man smelled of
hare. He came over, sniffed, wagged, and looked up into the
face under the fox hat, which meant, "I know, you're a hunter."

"You see?" Klim asked. "Blackie can tell who he's dealing
with. Sell him to me, I say."

"I won't. I won't sell him. I'll tell you something—even Alyosha didn't know about it at first—I sent three rubles to the
newspaper and ran an ad: 'Found: a hunting dog, white, with
a black ear.' I got an answer back: 'Don't advertise anymore,
please. Let it live with you until the time comes.' I don't know
what's going on, but I can tell that the dog is important and I
have to take care of it."

132

"You'll ruin it. Sell it," Klim insisted, getting angry.

"There will be no sale," Khrisan Andreyevich said. "If you want, you can take him out hunting and bring him back the same day. Let Blackie follow the calling of his breed, as he's supposed to."

"So he's not for sale," Alyosha added.

"Well, that's that," Klim concluded unhappily, scratched Beem's back, and left.

After supper, Khrisan Andreyevich went out with a lantern and slaughtered a sheep, skinned it, gutted it, and left the washed carcass to hang in the shed until morning.

Petrovna spent the evening packing eggs in a basket and filling jars with butter and chicken fat. She packed the jars in white market baskets.

And Beem realized that it all smelled of the city marketplace (the skinned sheep, the eggs, butter, and baskets). He should know! He knew the city from one end to the other, thanks to his search for Ivan Ivanovich. And Beem became excited. The market, the city, his own apartment—they all blended into one idea: Ivan Ivanovich was there. He didn't close his eyes all night.

Early in the morning, Khrisan Andreyevich wrapped the stiff carcass in clean burlap, tied it with cord, and heaved it over his shoulder. Petrovna balanced two baskets on a yoke over her shoulder. How Beem begged to go with them! He said it so clearly, explaining over and over, "I have to go with you. I'm going there, too. Take me."

No one understood his emotions. Even worse, Khrisan Andreyevich said, as he shifted the weight of the sheep on his back, "Alyosha, hold onto Blackie. I don't want him to run after us."

Alyosha held him by the collar and kept him on the porch. Papa and Mama, each with a heavy burden, slowly made their way to the highway and the bus stop. Beem followed them with his eyes, paying no attention to Alyosha's caresses and entreaties. He watched them until they were out of sight.

Klim showed up soon after, with his gun and backpack. He didn't have a game bag or cartridge belt (Beem noted the lack of proper equipment immediately). But still, he did have the gun!—and that's what counted. Beem reached out to the hunter trustingly and found out that the cartridges were in his pocket. That was very wrong, too. But he did have the gun. He would follow a man with a gun anywhere. Maybe not for long, but he would follow. He was a typical hunting dog when it came to guns, and he could discover the truth only through actual experience, even though he was the smartest of dogs. He still had much to go through just because he was a dog.

"Let's go hunting, Blackie," Klim said.

Beem jumped up and down: "Hunting, yes, hunting!"

Klim clipped on a leather leash, and Alyosha added, "Uncle Klim, when Blackie stands all stretched out, frozen, that's where the partridges are. You have to yell 'Scare 'em!' or he won't budge."

"Really?"

"Sure. I know," Alyosha explained with dignity. "I have homework to do, or I'd go show you."

"I know a thing or two myself. This isn't my first time," Klim assured him.

So, after a long break and many other experiences, Beem was going hunting. At first they didn't come upon anything but a skunk hole.

"Dig," Klim said.

Beem didn't understand commands like that, so he walked away and sat down in puzzlement.

It got warmer by midday. The sun melted the thin layer of snow, and mud squished under his feet, and the long hair on his legs got dirty and soggy, and Beem looked bedraggled and pathetic, like any wet setter. But he still sought according to all the rules—he went in front of Klim, then across his path, and then back to double-check. At the edge of a thicket, he threw a point at some partridges.

Klim shouted, "Scare 'em."

Beem jumped at the deep roar and flushed the partridges with a bark instead of the right way (what a big mistake!), but no shot followed. Beem turned. The hunter was stuffing a cartridge into his gun unsuccessfully. Then he tried to get it out, also unsuccessfully. Beem sat down, right on the spot where he had flushed the partridges, and watched the hunter. Klim was swearing the way drunks do on the street—reeling and swearing at each other or just into the black night. This one wasn't reeling, but he was swearing.

Even though Klim finally managed to extract the cartridge, insert another one, and close the gun, he was mad, and he reminded Beem of the Gray Man.

"Go seek!" he ordered. "Blackie, seek!"

Turning away and going out to seek against the wind, Beem pretended to do it. ("Well, I'll seek if you want.")

But there was something apathetic in his lame trot, and the excitement he had felt before flushing the partridges was gone. Klim mistook it for physical weakness, not understanding that in Beem it meant the beginning of his doubts about the man. He ran, giving the man sidelong glances, never stopping or coming too close, keeping a respectful distance. He didn't even seem to be seeking, only keeping an eye on the hunter, but that was an illusion. The unquenchable, unmanageable passion to hunt, which will exist as long as there are hunting dogs, won out. Basically, Beem was following the gun, not Klim.

Unexpectedly, he came on the scent of a hare. Ivan Ivanovich did not hunt these animals, even though Beem had pointed at them once or twice. After all, these hares don't stand still when you point—they just run off. And you can't run after them; his master didn't allow it. In the summer, of course, they do hold still a bit, but Ivan Ivanovich always called Beem off; and once

135

he removed a little bunny the size of his hand from under Beem's paw and set it free. A hare was no bird. But Beem set his nose on the scent coming from the hare, followed it precisely, and threw a point—wet and weak on one leg. No, a crippled dog doesn't have the right point. The artistry is gone.

"Scare 'em!" shouted Klim.

Let me add that in wet weather, especially in mud, a hare lies firm, and Beem hadn't moved from his point, as if to say, "You're yelling the wrong thing."

"Scare 'em, you lame devil!" Klim shouted.

Beem flushed the hare and lay down, the way you're supposed to before the shot.

Klim let it rip, like a cannon. The hare ran, but slower and slower. Then he sat, and then he hid in the brambles and disappeared from view.

Klim hooted, "I got 'im! Yay! I got 'im!" And ran in the direction of the hidden hare.

Even though he ran alongside Klim, Beem knew that things were being done incorrectly; the hunter isn't supposed to chase the game like a dog. Beem could find it himself if he had to— even a hare if Ivan Ivanovich ordered him to.

Klim stopped, out of breath, and shouted, "Seek, you idiot! Damned cripple!"

Beem went on, insulted. He wasn't all that interested in the hare scent in the first place, and now the man was stamping his feet behind him. But Beem followed the scent, found him, pointed, waited for the repulsive "Scare 'em," and jumped at the rabbit. The hare crawled out of the brambles and hobbled like a sick animal. Klim shot again, and the hare ran. Klim shot once more, and the hare hobbled on with short stops. Beem lay still, despite the mud, waiting for the command.

And Klim roared, "Get 'im! Go get 'im, you jerk!" And pointed at the hare.

Beem found the wounded hare's new hiding place and

pointed again. For the third time! And Klim missed again. And the hare ran off again.

In his anger, Klim couldn't understand that Blackie was not trained to destroy wounded game, that that was beneath the dignity of an intelligent setter, and that a setter despises hunters like him. When the hare hid for the last time (moving a little better—the wound must have been superficial), Klim became furious. He came right up to Beem and repeated the word "mother" a lot, angrily, with hatred. He was obviously cursing Beem.

Beem turned away, planning to leave the gun. And Klim kicked him with all his might, his huge boot striking Beem's chest.

Beem moaned. Like a human being.

"Oo-oh!" Beem called out and fell. "Ow, ow." Beem was speaking human language now. "Ow—why?" And he looked up in suffering, his tortured eyes questioning, not understanding, horrified.

Then he got up with difficulty, swayed, and collapsed, his legs twitching.

"What have I done!" Klim grabbed his head. "Now I'll have to give him the twenty-five rubles. The money's gone!" And he ran off very fast, running from Beem's eyes.

Klim did not show up in the village that day; he stayed out until nightfall. At midnight he crept through the gardens and into his house, which stood on the edge of the village.

But what about Beem? Where was he?

He was left alone on the cold, damp ground. Something had snapped inside from the blow and that "something" became warm, it took his breath away, gummed up his chest, and that's what made him black out. But he coughed, threw up, and took a breath—it hurt to breathe. He took another breath through his mouth and coughed. He raised his head with great effort— the field was moving, as though Beem were swimming in the

137

waves at high tide. He made an effort and sat up. The field swayed; the sun swayed as if it were suspended on a string.

Today more had been demanded of Beem than he could do. You must do this, they demanded, do what you can't do because it goes against your canine honor and conscience. And he was beaten viciously for not doing it. Beem would not allow a wounded animal to be torn to pieces.

"Why . . . why-y-y," Beem whimpered. "Where are you, my kind friend? Whe-ere? Where?" Beem cried more and more softly and gradually stopped.

There seemed to be a dead dog in a naked, muddy field. But that was not the case.

He raised his rear end, steadied himself, and didn't fall. He took a step—and didn't fall. He stood. Then he took another step. And made off down the field, dragging his feet, crisscrossing his own path.

What great courage and patience dogs have! What power made you so strong that even as you are dying you move your body forward? Just a little, but forward. Forward to a place where you might find trust and kindness for a pathetic, lonely, forgotten dog with a pure heart.

And Beem went on. Barely moving, he went on. Blood oozed from his mouth, but he went on. He coughed up blood, but he went on. He stumbled and fell to his knees, but he went on. He lay down weakly on the cold ground, got up, and went on some more.

He drank greedily at the brook—and felt a little better. Something told him not to leave the water. He made it to the nearest haystack, with barely enough strength to crawl under some protruding straw. This is the way dogs recuperate from illness, hiding from the eye of man and beast; nature taught them. Glory to its laws and purpose.

How long Beem lay unconscious he didn't know, but when he came to, he felt a searing pain in his chest; he was dizzy and,

138

sensing that something was about to happen to him, he climbed out of the straw. He lay in the open air. He could tell that his fur was now dry. He sat up. The autumn grass wasn't swaying anymore, the haystack wasn't swaying, nor was the sun, which was warm now. Beem straggled over to the brook and drank and drank. He rested a bit and then drank some more, taking smaller gulps now. He saw some steppe sedge growing nearby; it was stunted but still green (it withstood frost well). Beem began eating the sedge. What prompted him to eat that plain-looking grass is unknown—people can't even recognize it—but he knew that it was exactly what he needed. And he ate it. A tired, withered daisy, a chamomile plant, grew next to the sedge; he ate that, too. And then he returned to the brook, drank his fill, and went toward the village. He went on and on, always forward.

And he straggled in at twilight. No, Beem didn't enter the village. How could he! That's where Klim was. No, he wasn't about to follow him. Klim could get him by the collar again and then— No, that wouldn't happen to him.

Beem found himself a place in a leftover haystack, and rested. He smelled burdock growing near him, and he tasted it—it was dry, and he chewed the stem down to the ground and then worked on the root, getting under the soil. He also knew that he really needed to have burdock.

A dog's medical knowledge is extensive and varied. If you let a dog in the early stages of rabies go off into the woods, it will return in two or three weeks, emaciated, but cured. If a dog is having stomach problems, take it into the woods or the steppes and live with it there for two or three days. It'll cure itself with herbs and grasses.

The night passed. A big, autumnal night that gnawed at his insides.

The first roosters crowed. Beem didn't wait for the second and third ones, the ones that crowed at dawn. He got up but couldn't move because of the pain in his chest. But with effort he got rid of some of the stiffness in his muscles, by lying down and standing up twice, and he moved on slowly.

He reached Khrisan Andreyevich's house, climbed the two steps to the porch, and lay down. The house was silent.

Who knows, he might never have left there that day, but Klim passed close by, too close, steathily, like a thief. Beem shivered. He was prepared to defend himself to the death. The pride of the doomed came to him, when there was nothing more to lose. But Klim leaned over the railing and whispered, "You're back, Blackie." And he crept off quickly, like a coward, apparently in a better mood.

Beem didn't have the strength to catch up with him and avenge the cruel kick, and he couldn't bark because all that came out was a painful rattle. But he didn't want Klim to return suddenly and try to get him. And so he got up, quietly circled the yard, sniffing the pigs and the cow and the sheep, sat for a bit, and left the village. He had wanted to lie down with his piglet friends so much!

The third rooster crowed. It was dawn.

A dog was heading for the highway. Head down, tail tucked between its legs, the dog looked rabid. It looked as if it were in the last stages of the disease and would collapse as soon as it came upon an obstacle, collapse and drop dead on the spot. That was our Beem, our kind and faithful Beem. He was on his way to look for his master, Ivan Ivanovich. He followed the path by which he had been brought here.

It was two or three miles from the village to the bus stop, but Beem lost his strength along the way, and he barely made it to a haystack. Someone stealing hay in the night had made a hole in the stack, and Beem climbed into it. He lay there for a long time, almost the whole day, and came out just before sunset. He was thirsty, but there was no water. The pain was wracking his chest, but he could breathe more easily and he was no longer

140

dizzy when he walked. He came across a clump of everlastings, and he ate some of the flowers, the dry yellow flowers that don't change color from the time they bloom through the whole winter. And he picked at a bush of chamomile, but the flowers were ripe here and crumbled in his mouth, choking him and making him even thirstier. When he was crossing one of the back roads, he came across a puddle of melted snow. So the road had saved some water for Beem. He drank and went on his way.

He got to the highway after dark. He sat for a while watching the cars whizz by with their blinding lights, and he knew he had to go. But at night? What if he ran into Klim? Or the Gray Man? Or a wolf?

Beem decided to stay close to the road and hide nearby for the night. He reached the bus stop, which had a three-sided shelter with a wide bench; he huddled in the corner under the bench and waited.

He didn't sleep a wink all night, despite his terrible weakness. Cars drove by—the road was alive even at night. The bus slowed but didn't stop because there were no passengers waiting.

The night was tense and wary and painful, but at least it was warm; thank God, autumn had chased winter away once more.

What had happened back in the village in the twenty-four hours Beem was gone?

Khrisan Andreyevich and Petrovna returned from the market at dusk. Alyosha wasn't home; the house was locked. They came in, counted the money they had made in the city, put it away in the trunk for now, planning to take it to the savings association in the morning. Alyosha came home.

"Where were you?" his father asked.

"I was over at Klim's."

"Didn't he return Blackie?"

"He's not back from hunting yet."

141

"He'll be back. And he'll bring Blackie back. He's not going to disappear anywhere," Petrovna said soothingly, holding a new sweater up to Alyosha's chest.

"You would think so," Khrisan Andreyevich said doubtfully, "but Klim's a thief. At least if he only stole from the kolkhoz—that stuff is nobody's—but he steals from the kolkhoz farmers. He's a tough one to get mixed up with. Everyone's afraid of him. He can take Blackie out hunting if he wants.

"What do you mean, 'nobody's'?" Alyosha asked. "It's ours, isn't it?"

"Sure, you're right. I didn't mean that. You're right, it's ours. But, let's see, what's the best way to explain this? That stuff is ours, but things here are our own. Let's put it this way. For instance, the school is ours, and all the children are ours, but you are my own. Or: the fields are ours, and the garden is our own. And the same goes for the livestock; some is ours, and some is our own. Understand?"

"Sure! It's easy. But you said 'nobody's.' "

"You're right. Nothing can be absolutely nobody's at all."

Alyosha's father always treated him like an adult. Alyosha responded in kind.

"So, what you meant about Klim was that you'd rather he stole from ours than from our own."

"I guess you're right. But you and I, we take from the common goods—some hay or some beet leaves for the cow, don't we? We do. And we don't tell the kolkhoz chairman. But he knows, and the brigade leader knows, everyone knows. And you can't get away from it—we take from our stores. And we don't overdo it; we take from last year's haystacks or we pick the leftover beets. How else could we manage? We have to take care of the livestock."

"That's so," said the boy, who at thirteen knew how to herd, and how to take care of "his own" cattle, and how to churn butter to help his mother when he was free, and how to clean "our" beets in the freezing cold, and how to dig "our own" potatoes.

Khrisan Andreyevich explained some more. "We all live according to the regulations—that is ours, and this is mine. I brought a sheep to the city. And why not? Those people have to eat, too—that's our job. And your mother brought eggs to sell. And butter. All regulation, all in the plan. Life is good now, Alyosha, we have clothes and shoes that are no worse than those of a professor or a chairman. We have a TV and all those things, and money when we need it. And having to work hard for it, well, that just makes us stronger—no harm in that. Just don't you drink vodka," he added.

"You drink it," Alyosha noted reasonably. "If it's so bad, you shouldn't do it, either."

"You're right again. But you do have to have a few drinks to toast the brigade leader when he drops by—that's a custom that was started way before our time. But as for Klim—he's nothing but a thief. How can a man steal a chicken from his neighbor? That means he's lost his conscience completely. No, that man's no man."

Waiting up for Blackie to return, Khrisan Andreyevich and Alyosha talked until eleven. Then they searched the yard, looked in the pigsty, under the porch (maybe he ran away from Klim and hid here?). Finally Khrisan Andreyevich went to Klim's himself.

Natalya, Klim's wife, quiet and browbeaten by her husband, was the same sad woman who had cried at the beet field. She said, "He's not back yet, the bum. He's spending the night somewhere, the brute. Or else he's drunk. Oh, that man! He won't be back till morning, I guess. But he won't do anything to the dog, don't worry about that. I know him. He'll bring the dog back."

Khrisan Andreyevich came home, told Alyosha what she had said, and the two went to bed, whispering, so as not to wake up

143

Mama. They didn't hear Beem come to the porch, or Klim creep up and run away, or their new friend go away from the evil man.

In the morning, Alyosha was awakened by his father.

"Get up. There are fresh tracks on the porch. Blackie is back."

The two of them looked all over, calling and whistling, but Blackie couldn't hear them by now. Khrisan Andreyevich ran over to Klim's and woke him up.

"I brought him back, I did," Klim said in a hoarse, grumpy voice. "I brought him back after midnight, and I didn't want to wake you up. I'll show you my footprints if you want. But you woke me up. Do you think that's a nice thing to do? And your stupid dog is no good for hunting, anyway. I don't know where I got it into my head—I'll never take him out again."

Khrisan Andreyevich didn't argue; he didn't want to get mixed up with him.

Alyosha and his father looked all over the village and checked the kolkhoz yards (maybe Blackie was visiting the dogs there?). No, no one had seen Blackie at all. Blackie was gone.

"Klim must have beaten him, and Blackie ran away," Khrisan Andreyevich guessed.

Alyosha's heart was filled with pity and sorrow. He examined the porch floorboards; the tracks had dried, but you could still see the spot where Blackie had lain. Alyosha bent over and then raced into the house with a cry: "Papa! There's blood!"

His father ran out to look. The area under Blackie's head was covered with stains of saliva mixed with blood.

"The beast!" said Khrisan Andreyevich. He warned Alyosha, "Stay clear of him—he's trouble. Listen, let's follow Blackie's path—I know how he would go."

They got all the way to the bus stop, calling Blackie along the way, waited there for a long time, and then went home. They decided that if he had come this way, he was now long gone.

144

They had passed the haystack where Blackie had rested, where Beem had rested.

In the evening, Alyosha went out several times to call Blackie from the porch. And then he sat down by the kennel stuffed with hay and cried openly, sobbing and smearing his disobedient tears with his sleeve.

Khrisan Andreyevich heard him. He came out and turned on the light. "Are you crying, my son?" He was surprised.

"Yes, I am," Alyosha replied with a shudder.

He stroked the boy's hair with his rough, heavy hand. "You're a good boy, Alyosha, a kind heart. Go ahead and cry."

Petrovna came out, too. "Missing Blackie, are you?"

"Oh, Mama! I'm so sorry he's gone."

"What a pity, dear," she said, sobbing herself. "There's nothing we can do now, Alyosha. That's all. What a shame."

And at that very moment, Beem was lying under the bench at the bus stop.

He was lying and waiting. He was waiting for only one thing —the dawn.

13

THE FOREST HOSPITAL, MAMA AND PAPA, AND A FOREST STORM

At dawn's first glimmer, Beem tried to get up, but it was hard, almost impossible to get out of his rolled-up position. Something had stiffened inside; it felt glued together. He stretched one leg —not at all like a dog, but like a chicken extending a leg from under her wing—and then the other, pushed against the wall, and crawled out from under the bench. He lay still for a while and then inched out of the booth. He sat down. The circulation was returning to his numb legs. Overcoming his pain and whining softly to himself, he went on—first with great difficulty, dragging his feet, and then more easily.

He tried a slow trot, and that eased the pain in his chest. And so he trotted along, gently. He was neither running nor walking, just moving his legs without moving his body. That made it easier. The herbs and the motion made him feel better. And so he trotted along.

He traveled on the left side of the road—facing the oncoming traffic. He certainly didn't know the "Traffic Regulations for the Roads of the USSR." And there was no logic in his decision, as it might have appeared to those drivers who saw him. No, it was only that he had been brought to the village on this side of the road, and that's the way he went back. People flashing by in car windows thought, What a smart dog—obeying the rules of the road. But it's sick.

Beem went on for a long time—three or four hours (it was longer, of course, if you counted the rest stops). He never went much faster than a pedestrian, but that was pretty good for him!

And suddenly, unexpectedly, he recognized the bus stop where they always got off when they went hunting! He recognized it.

There were people at the stop waiting for a bus. Beem halted some way off and turned left onto the road they took to get to the forest. Someone whistled and someone called to him and someone else shouted, "Rabid dog!" Beem didn't pay any attention. He even tried to run faster, shifting to a gallop, but he couldn't move any faster, and the effort made it harder to move at all.

The important thing was to get there. Where Ivan Ivanovich might have been recently or would soon be. Hurry, forward.

Beem jogged toward the forest. He stopped at the edge, looked around, and went in. He quickly found the familiar clearing and stood by a stump. He stood, sniffed all around without moving, and then circled the stump, nose to the ground. And suddenly, decisively, he lay down on the leaves by the stump. It was here, right here, that Ivan Ivanovich always sat before starting to hunt. Beem stretched out his neck and rubbed his head in the yellow leaves on the spot where his friend's feet had once stood, even though all traces of Ivan Ivanovich's scent had been blown away by the wind long ago.

And the day was so warm!

There are days in late autumn, even after a frost, when summer returns and touches departing autumn with its fiery tail. And autumn melts, gentles, and quiets down, like a cuddly dog caressed by a woman. And then the forest is redolent of the farewell fragrances of fallen leaves, the ruby sweetbrier hips and the amber bayberries, the pungent, sharp ginger and the untouched, crumbling, waterlogged white mushroom, reminiscent of other seasons. And the smiling sweet scent of pine will stretch to the birch, and from the birch to the oak, which will respond with the fragrance of power, woodsy strength, and eternity. There is something eternal and indestructible in forest scents that is felt particularly on the warm, gentle days of autumn's farewell; by then, autumn has freed herself of the dreary rains, the vicious attacks of cold, and the nauseating, persistent hoarfrost. Everything is gone, in the past, and it's as if autumn, falling asleep, dreams of summer and displays her divine visions in all their glory of animate beauty and vibrant odors of the earth. Blessed is he who has captured all this in childhood and manages to carry it throughout his life without spilling a drop.

On days like this, the forest becomes all-forgiving, though demanding. Tranquil, you become one with nature. During these solemn moments of autumn's dreams, you wish that there were no lies and evil in the world. And in the silence of departing autumn, enchanted by her gentle dreaminess, in these days of brief oblivion of the winter to come, you begin to understand: there must be only truth, only honor, only a clear conscience, and it must be spoken about.

Perhaps that is why I write about the fate of a dog, about its devotion, honor, and loyalty. About the dog that lay on that very warm autumn day beside a stump in the forest. And pined.

Thus, on one of nature's most beautiful days, miserable Beem lay in the forest. And the day was so warm!

But the ground was cold. That was why Beem had curled up for a rest by the stump, as if at his master's feet, and had then gone on into the forest, looking for something. He was hungry. He came across a freshly fallen poplar and chewed its juicy bark, the favorite food of the elk. Did Beem suspect that this bark was also good medicine for him?

148

It must be the dog's subtle sense of smell that helps him distinguish between helpful and harmful herbs. After all, Beem certainly wouldn't eat poisonous ginger, but he did stop at a valerian root. He dug a bit in the soft, friable earth, gnawed off the root, and ate it. And then he had some more. The valerian root is easy to get at; it grows almost at the surface. He ate just as much as he needed, not a tiny bit more, and circled, as if to prepare a spot to lie down in, but the place didn't suit him (we don't know why). So he searched some more until he came upon an old wartime trench filled with soft leaves, and he went down there, circling to make another bed. He made a deep and soft one; yet he didn't seem to want to lie down, and he fought sleep; but finally he collapsed into it and slept immediately.

The valerian had done its work. It's called wild chervil in the Tambov region; no healthy dog will eat it in any region, though he might sniff it or rub his face in it; but the sick ones eat it. And so Beem ate it. And I beg of you, be quiet. Very quiet. Beem is sleeping in that hole.

He had eaten nothing but herbs for three days and gone without sleep because of the pain and tension; certainly he hadn't slept so soundly in a long time. It was quiet and warm in the hole, and the forest, autumnally hushed, guarded Beem's peace and quiet, healed him with herbs and healthful air.

Beem awoke toward evening. He climbed out. It was still painful to walk, but much easier than it had been in the morning. His insides were better. But he was still weak. He went back to the old stump, sat for a while, and then returned to his bed. And sat some more. And checked with his nose and looked around. Everything was quiet. And he went back to sleep in his cozy, warm hole.

And he slept through the entire night. And didn't get chilled.

He was awakened at dawn by a gentle rustle. He looked up and listened; someone was digging around in the leaves. Beem

149

crawled out and read the air with his nose. He learned that it was a woodcock.

The irresistible urge to hunt strengthened his weakened body and silenced the pressing pain. The woodcock was no more than five feet away from him. The bird was tearing through the leaves with its feet, sticking its nose into the soft earth, accurately aiming for the tunnel of an earthworm, pulling the worm out, and eating it with pleasure. The bird was dragging a wing (that's what happens to the wounded victims of bad hunters; they survive until winter and then either become a fox's meal or die, if they manage to last until the severe frosts).

Beem took a step—the woodcock, engrossed in his work, didn't hear. He took another—it still was too busy working. The woodcock can't afford to lose time. The warm weather brings worms up to the surface; sometimes they crawl out of the earth and live under the leaves. Beem crept up on it from behind a tree and froze in a point. No one shouted "Forward!" but Beem moved on his own. He wanted to pounce on the bird and hold it down with his paws, but he couldn't jump; he simply fell and grabbed the woodcock with his teeth. He held it until he turned over on his stomach and—he ate it. He ate the entire bird, leaving only feathers. He even ate the beak, which, he discovered, was soft.

How could this have happened? How could Beem, a dog trained by an experienced hunter, violate the code of honor and eat game? It happened because a dog wants to live.

His strength was coming back. He was thirsty, and he found a puddle, in which any hospitable forest abounds, and slaked his thirst. On the way back, he picked up the scent of a mouse. He ate that, too, a little snack. And then he looked for herbs. He pulled out some wild garlic, spitting out the greens. He ate the bulb, making a face (it was garlic, after all). He wandered in the forest, picking up what he needed. God only knows how Beem

knew that garlic is two- or three-tenths of a percent iodine. I can
only suppose that in his difficult, almost final hours a few days
earlier, the vast experience of his ancestors, programmed into
his genes long ago, was revealed to him in a flash.

Beem continued curing himself for five days. He ate whatever came his way, but he was assiduous in his medication. He
slept in the hole, which had become a temporary home for him.
Once he came upon a sleeping hare, but he didn't catch it; the
hare leaped up and ran off. Beem didn't try to chase him—a
healthy setter couldn't catch him, and there was no point in a
sick one even trying. He watched him bound off and licked his
chops. But the forest didn't hurt Beem; he always found something to eat—not very much, but enough. He had lost weight
from his illness and the lack of food, but the herbs did their
work. Beem not only survived, but he was well enough to continue his task of looking for his human friend.

On one routine check of the clearing with the stump, Beem
lay down, got up, lay down, and got up again. He must have
decided that Ivan Ivanovich wasn't coming back there. He
went back to the hole, and then back to the stump; he stopped
for a moment at each place and moved on. This running back
and forth was evidence of great impatience; his agitation was
increasing. Finally he ran past the stump without stopping and
trotted out to the highway. It was getting on toward evening,
when the sun was preparing to go rest.

Beem got into town late in the evening. It was light in the
city, not like the forest at night, and this light disturbed Beem.
He had never felt like that. He was walking carefully and yet
hurriedly, as fast as his health permitted, headed for home, of
course, to his master, to Stepanovna, to Lusya, to Tolik—they
must all be there. But on the outskirts of town, among those
carbon-copy houses, Beem decided to circle the neighborhood
so as to avoid the Gray Man's house. He turned down a side

street and came upon a fence. He followed it for a bit, and at the gate he found Tolik's scent! The boy whom Beem had grown to love had walked by here. Recently. The gate was locked, but Beem, without giving it a second thought, squeezed under the gate and followed his friend's trail. He had just walked here! It was a tiny garden, and there was a small two-story house in the middle. The trail went inside.

Beem approached the door that Tolik had just passed through. Trained to trust doors from early puppyhood, Beem scratched at this one. There was no answer. Beem didn't realize that this kind of behavior might be described as the insolence of the naive. But he scratched again, louder this time.

A woman's voice called out from behind the door, "Who is it?"

"Me," said Beem. "Woof!"

"What nonsense is this? Tolik! There's someone here to see you with a dog. That's all I need."

"It's me, me!" Beem said. "Woof woof!"

"Beem! Beem!" Tolik shouted and opened the door. "Beem! Darling, dearest Beem!" And he hugged him.

Beem licked the boy's hands, jacket, and slippers and kept looking into his eyes. How much hope, faith, and love were in the eyes of the dog that had suffered so much!

"Mama, Mama, look at his eyes. They're human! Beem, smart Beem, you found me yourself. Mother, he found me on his own."

Tolik's mother didn't say a word while the friends were having their joyous reunion. But when the ecstasy had died down a little, she asked, "Is it the same one?"

"Yes. This is Beem. He's a good dog."

"Throw it out immediately!"

"Mama!"

"Right now!"

Tolik hugged Beem closely.

152

"Don't, Mama, please!" And he began to cry.

The door chimes rang. A man came in. He spoke in a tired but kind voice.

"What's all the yelling? Are you crying, Tolik?" He took off his coat and shoes, put on slippers, and said, "Well, what's the matter, silly?" He stroked Tolik's hair and tugged at Beem's ear. "So, so. A little dog. Look at the doggie—skinny."

"Papa, he's a good dog, he's Beem. Don't."

Mama was screaming now. "It's always this way. I tell him one thing, you say the opposite. You call that bringing him up? You're going to ruin him! You'll tear your hair out, but it'll be too late!"

"Wait a minute, wait, don't shout. Calm down." He led her into another room, where she shouted even louder while he tried to quiet her down.

Beem understood that Mama was against Beem and Papa was for him, and that for now he would stay with Tolik. A person would have understood even if his ears had been plugged. And Beem was a dog with unplugged ears and wise eyes. Of course he understood! And Tolik led Beem into his own room (it smelled only of Tolik in there).

Neither Beem nor Tolik heard the rest of his parents' conversation.

"Why do you say things like 'You'll ruin the child' in front of Tolik? It's bad for him!"

"And this isn't? The dog is obviously sick, a stray, and you want it here in our spotless house? Are you mad? He'll come down with some disease he picks up from that dog by tomorrow! I won't allow it! Throw that mutt out immediately!"

"Ah, some mother you are," Semyon Petrovich sighed. "You haven't the slightest idea of tactics."

"You know what you can do with your tactics."

"There you go again. This has to be done wisely. We have to keep from traumatizing Tolik and still get rid of the dog." He

153

whispered something to her and then said, "That's how we'll get rid of it."

"You should have said so in the first place," Mama said.

"I couldn't in front of Tolik. And you, you little fool, you make fun of my tactics." He caressed her cheek.

They entered Tolik's room, and Mama said, "Well, he can stay, I guess."

"Sure, let him stay."

Tolik was overjoyed. He looked gratefully at his parents, and he told them all about Beem and showed them all his tricks.

It was a happy family scene, a family in which everyone was pleased with life.

"But only under one condition, Tolik. Beem will sleep in the entry, and under no circumstances will he sleep with you," Papa said.

"All right, sure," Tolik said. "He is very clean, you know. I know him well."

Beem decided that Papa was a good, calm, steady, and confident man. And when, a little later, Tolik took Beem on a tour of the house, Beem noticed that Papa ate alone, reading the paper, and that he did that calmly and confidently, too. He was a good man, Papa—also known as Semyon Petrovich.

Tolik worked with Beem until late—combed him, fed him a little (Papa said not to overfeed him—"A starved dog can die if you give him too much too fast"), and wheedled a mattress from his mother (a brand-new one!), which he set up in a corner of the entry.

"This is your place, Beem. Go to your place!"

Beem lay down without an argument. He understood it all— that was where he would live for now. He felt warmed by the kindness and attention of the boy.

"It's time for bed, Tolik. It's ten-thirty already. Time for bed, son," Papa said.

Tolik got into bed. Falling asleep, he thought, Tomorrow I'll go see Stepanovna and tell her to let Beem live with me until Ivan Ivanovich returns. And then he remembered that when he told his parents that he visited Stepanovna and there was a little girl there named Lusya, and he walked Beem, Mama had begun screaming and Papa had said, "You won't go there any-more." And when Tolik had started to cry, Papa had said to Mama, "We forgot about tactics." And he had stroked Tolik's hair and said, "Well, what can you do? You have to grow up and become a man, and you can't be a dog handler and spend your time visiting old ladies. What can you do? That's the way it is!" But now Beem would live at his house, and he wouldn't have to go visit "old ladies." He'd just run down to Stepanovna's once, to tell her everything. And to see Lusya. What a nice girl she was. And Beem must be asleep. Good Beem . . .

And with that thought, Tolik fell into a calm, happy, and delightful sleep.

In the middle of the night, Beem heard footsteps. He opened his eyes, without raising his head, and watched. Papa went over to the phone quietly, stood and listened for a second, and then lifted the receiver and whispered, "Bring the car—now."

Naturally, Beem didn't know those words. But he noticed that Papa kept looking anxiously at Tolik's door and casting nervous glances at Beem, then he went into the kitchen and came out with a rope and a package. Beem saw that something was wrong and that something had changed in Papa—he didn't seem himself. An inner voice told him to bark and run to Tolik, and Beem would have done just that, but Papa came over and petted him (that meant everything was fine), tied the rope to his collar, put on an overcoat, opened the door quietly, and took Beem outside.

A car was purring at the curb.

Beem rode in the back seat. There was a man at the wheel, and Papa sat beside him. The package on the seat next to Beem smelled of meat. The rope was around his neck. The people were silent. So was Beem. It was night. A very dark night. The sky was covered with clouds. The sky was as black as the cast-iron pots in Khrisan Andreyevich's house. A dog can't follow the road from a car and remember the way back on a night like that. And Beem didn't know where they were taking him. That wasn't his concern. They were taking him somewhere, and that was that. But what was the rope for? Beem gave in to his anxiety when they got to the forest and stopped.

Semyon Petrovich, carrying a gun, led Beem deep into the forest. They went down into a ravine, lighting their way with a flashlight. The path led to a small clearing surrounded by huge oaks. Semyon Petrovich tied Beem to a tree, opened the package, and removed a bowl of meat, which he put in front of Beem. He didn't say a word. And he left. But after taking a few steps, he turned back, blinding Beem with his flashlight, and said, "You're on your own. Good luck."

Beem watched the beam of light disappear, and said nothing —he was shocked, amazed, and bitterly hurt. He didn't understand a single thing about this. And he quivered tensely, even though it was warm, even stuffy—very unusual for autumn.

The car drove off. Beem knew which way it went by the receding sound of the motor, growing fainter and fainter; the sound told Beem which way to go, if he had to.

The forest was silent.

In the deep, dark autumn night, a dog sat among the mighty trees, tied up with a rope.

And it had to happen just that night! It happens rarely, but it happens—at the end of November, in such unusually warm temperatures, thunder rumbles off in the distance.

At first Beem sat and listened to the forest, checking it as far as he could. It's not hard for a dog to determine which forest he's in, if he's ever been there before. Beem soon realized that he was where he and his master had once gone to round up wolves. The very same forest. But now there was no scent of

156

wolf nearby. Beem huddled up to the tree, cringing in the impenetrable darkness, blending into it, a solitary, defenseless dog, abandoned there by a man to whom he had never done any harm.

Inside, deep in the fiber of his being, Beem understood that he shouldn't go back to Tolik and that he had to go to his own door now, there and nowhere else. And he longed to be there so much that he forgot about the rope and ran; the rope held him back, and he fell. The pain in his chest spread throughout his body. He lay still, all four legs extended. But that didn't last long, and he got up again and sat by the tree, seemingly resigned to his fate.

Thunder roared again in the black night, closer this time, and resounded heavily through the leafless forest. The wind blew, making the branches moan as if they sensed impending disaster, the weaker tree trunks swayed, and finally all the noises blended into a single menacing black sound. The creak of a desiccated aspen could be heard above it; it creaked rhythmically somewhere near its roots, cracked and exhausted; and its hollow, dreary creak frightened Beem more than the sounds of the whole forest.

And the forest roared on. And the wind got stronger, the sovereign of the darkness, so strong that the oak began to groan. Beem thought that someone very black and huge had spread himself over the powerful oaks, over the hopeless, dying aspen, over him, a poor dog lost among the harsh elements. And this black monster slashed at the treetops with his cloak, catching the trees in his mad embrace and shaking them in a wild dance, whirling and twitching like a shaman, screaming and howling with a hundred voices.

Beem was so terrified that the pain in his body receded. He pressed himself to the tree, glued himself to it. The wind brought cold into the forest, and a chilling stream of air poured through the ravine, immediately penetrating Beem. Harsh cold always comes hard upon warm weather this late in the year. Beem moved to the other side of the tree, out of the wind; he wanted to be downwind to catch scents and see the way the wind was blowing. But the darkness was impenetrable. He was shaking.

Suddenly, like a thin, fiery blade, lightning split the darkness, illuminating the wild, howling forest, and then something exploded up above, rattled in a million broken pieces, surged down, and rolled in every direction through the forest. The thunder and lightning seemed to scare off the shaman, who started to run and then disappeared completely; and then drops pounded from above. The rain was brief, violent, and cold. And then it stopped, too.

The forest grumbled softly, shaking and righting itself, as if after battle. But suddenly the aspen creaked and cracked, grabbing onto the other trees, bidding farewell to its neighbors, and crashed to the earth with a sickening thud, breaking its branches in bitter predeath hopelessness. It lived through its last battle and fell. The aspen was close to Beem, and he was frightened by the sounds of the tree's death and the way it seemed to be falling right on him; he backed away from his oak tree as the aspen fell, pulling the rope taut—but the rope held.

Beem sat there until dawn, soaked, sick, exhausted. The bowl of meat was in front of him—he hadn't touched it.

A wolf howled in the distance just before dawn. There was only one wolf; there were no others to answer his call. It was the crafty old wolf that had escaped the roundup. Beem's fur bristled, his teeth chattering, and he listened, sniffing the air, inhaling deeply. He was prepared for the encounter, not even aware that he had the courage to defend himself—which could be called the heroism of desperation (after all, he had bitten the Gray Man, almost knocking him off his feet!). But the wolf didn't come this time. There was no wind, so the beast couldn't tell Beem was there, and it evidently wasn't time for it to prowl in

158

this part of the forest. But Beem's tension had caused him to pull the rope so tight that it was choking him. He backed up to the tree, pressed his rear end against the trunk, got the rope between his molars, and bit through it. Clean as a knife!

It was done!

Beem was free, but alone in the deep forest.

Every dog will do this sooner or later, though when it does so varies with the breed. Those kept on chains will chew through a rope immediately; a lap dog will not bite through a rope, but will struggle against it, twisting and yelping, and may end up choking itself; a hound will give it a lot of thought before finally doing it; an intelligent dog that works real game will spend many days waiting for its master, but will bite through the rope in a moment of danger or despair, when it becomes clear that no one will come to help. And so it was with Beem; the time came, and he did what he had to do.

He walked away from the tree cautiously, listening carefully. A magpie chattered nearby, "Someone's here-here-here! Someone's here-here-here! Near-near-near!" At the magpie's first warning, Beem instantly stopped, in a thicket of new oaks surrounding a sturdy centegenarian. He hardly felt the pain at all anymore; it had gone deep inside. He lay down on the carpet of leaves, stretching out his neck and pressing his head to the ground. The magpie had called out close by—Beem saw it in a tall tree. He would have left without wasting a minute, but the magpie was warning him of danger in the direction in which he was headed. He waited nervously, yet with determination, and with gratitude to the magpie. Only beasts of prey disparage this bird, the marvelous town crier, born with a telegraph key for a tail, a volunteer on behalf of the peaceful inhabitants of the forest.

A she-wolf came to the edge of the clearing and stopped. Her foreleg was crooked (it must have been wounded by man). Limping, she took a few more steps, turned her head straight

159

at Beem, and—took a flying leap in his direction. But she missed; her crippled leg let her down. Beem got away from her at the very last moment, jumping to one side. The beast, turning and seeming to jump on three legs, attacked him again. He rolled behind the oak and felt an opening with his back. And at the very moment of the she-wolf's second miss, he squeezed into the hollow trunk, bared his teeth, growled, and began barking as he had never barked before—like a hound running with a pack, like a husky at a bear's den, without taking a breath. Beem's voice rang out through the forest in one word, understood by everyone: "Trouble!" "Trouble!" And the forest picked up the cry: "Trouble!" "Trouble!"

And the alarming news passed from magpie to magpie, faster than any telegraph: "Someone's eating someone, someone's eating someone, oh-oh, oh-oh-oh." The forest ranger decided that the barking and the magpie chatter meant trouble. He picked up his gun, loaded it, and went into the forest. The man moved boldly because the forest was a second home to him, and the forest creatures knew him well. And he knew many of them; he knew the she-wolf, but for some reason he didn't kill her. Could some young hunter have wandered into the she-wolf's territory, been frightened by her, and climbed up a tree, leaving his dog to be torn to pieces? he thought, increasing his speed. The barking was coming from far away, at the very end of Wolf Ravine, but stopped abruptly. "It's done for!" he decided and went on more slowly. Ah, he should have hurried. Hurried!

What had happened?

The she-wolf was experienced; she moved away from the tree to make Beem stop barking, because she knew that a barking dog always brought a man with a gun. Beem stopped because she was no longer attacking him. In a little while, she moved closer and sat, never taking her eyes off him. And so two dogs looked each other in the eye: a wild dog, a distant relative of

160

Beem's, and man's enemy, and an intelligent dog that couldn't live without man's kindness; the wolf hates all men, and Beem would have loved them all if they had all been kind to him. One dog—the friend of man—and another dog—the enemy of man —looked into each other's eyes.

The she-wolf knew that she couldn't fit through the opening of the hollow trunk, but she approached it, anyway, sticking her muzzle in. Beem backed up, baring his teeth, but he didn't bark because he knew he was untouchable in his fortress.

It's impossible to know how long this would have continued. But the she-wolf sniffed around, turned sharply from the tree, and, crouching as if to ward off danger, moved step by step toward the clearing, to the oak where Beem had been tied. She went there in terror, her tail hanging straight down.

She had missed that spot in the heat of her hunt for Beem and because the night rain had washed away most of the smells, but now with the light wind, she discovered them: the rope on the tree, the bowl of meat. Oh, she knew what they meant: man had been here! The rope smelled of man, the round thing smelled of iron, and there were *his* footprints; the meat was a trick, a trap. She stopped, then leaped to the side and ran away from a great trap. That's how a wolf runs from a trap laid by someone who doesn't know how—a trap that is not camouflaged and that smells of man.

The last she-wolf in the forest, brave and proud, ran from Beem.

The only creature on earth that the wolf hates is man. The last wolves are treading this earth, and you, man, will kill them, kill these freedom-loving workers of forest and field, cleansing the earth of vermin, carrion, and disease, regulating life so that only healthy progeny are left. The last wolves walk the earth. They stalk to destroy the mangy fox, safeguarding others from contagion; to destroy tapeworm-infested hares so that they do not spread their disease in the forest and fields and breed sickly

161

offspring; to annihilate vast numbers of mice in years when they carry tularemia. The last wolves are walking the earth.

When they howl, sad and lonely in the night, your soul, man, contracts and shivers at the frank statement: "I-ii-i am! I am!" And yet you know that a she-wolf will not harm a suckling puppy but will adopt it; and she will not harm an infant but will take it to her lair and nudge it toward her teats. How many instances there have been of wolves bringing up human infants! Jackals can't do that. Even dogs can't. And will a wolf touch a sheep in its homeground? Never. But you still fear them. Thus hatred, overcoming reason, can overpower you and make you think that the benign is harmful, and vice versa.

But for a while longer, the last wolves still walk the earth.

One of them ran from the hated and dangerous smell of man, but not from Beem. Who knows how their encounter would have ended and how long the wolf would have stayed by the tree? Perhaps they would have come to terms (she was alone, and Beem was a male). Men have seen dogs running with more than one wolf pack. But Beem was spared that fate.

After the she-wolf ran off, a sharp pain again seared Beem's chest. He began to choke, crawled out of the tree trunk, and fell to the ground. And he still rejected the meat even after he had rested and could stand again. There was only one thing to do: go forward as far as his strength would take him.

And Beem went on. He scrambled up the long, half-mile slope slowly and painfully. About halfway up, he stumbled on the she-wolf's trail and didn't dare cross it (she had come from this direction, after all!), and so he turned into the thick brambles and—saw a wolf. Right in front of his face, but dead. It was the mortally wounded wolf that had escaped the roundup, by whose side the she-wolf had remained, her sorrow expressed in the lonely howls man finds so terrifying. The wolf was dead. His fur was falling off in patches. There was only part of the disintegrating animal left. The claws had become long, evilly clean,

162

and horrible. Beem saw that even a dead, rotten wolf retains his claws. And they scared him.

Beem hurried back to the path as fast as he could, avoiding the scent that had made him get off it.

Finally he reached the top, stopped at the spot where the car had parked yesterday, looked around, and went in exactly the right direction—homeward. And when his strength left him, he rested—in a haystack, in a pine thicket—and he looked for herbs along the way.

An emaciated, limping dog ran along the highway. It ran forward, always forward, slowly, with difficulty, but ever forward to the door where there was kindness, where Beem wanted to lie down and wait, wait, wait for his master, wait for trust and the most ordinary, simple human kindness.

And what about Tolik? What happened to him after he woke up?

Still in his underwear, he ran out to see Beem and began shouting, "Mama! Where's Beem? Where is he?"

Mama calmed him down. "Beem wanted to pee. Papa let him out, and he didn't come back. He ran away. Papa called and called, but he ran away."

"Papa!" Tolik cried. "It's not true, it's not, it's not!" He threw himself down on his bed, still in his underwear, and cried with reproach, with entreaty, with the hope that it wasn't true. "It's not true, it's not, it's not!"

Now Semyon Petrovich tried consoling Tolik. "He'll come back, he will. And if he doesn't, we'll go find him ourselves. And bring him back. Yes, we will. We'll find him. A dog isn't a needle in a haystack."

Tolik stopped crying and stared into space. Then he looked at his parents, dried his tears, and said, "I'll find him, anyway."

He spoke with such determination that his parents exchanged a nervous look, their eyes saying, "He has a mind of his own."

From that day on, Tolik became very quiet at home and in school, withdrawn, suspicious of his nearest and dearest.

He looked for Beem. A frequent sight in the city was a neat little boy from a happy, cultured family stopping a passerby, picked at random, and asking him, "Mister, have you seen a white dog with one black ear?"

14

THE ROAD TO HIS OWN DOOR, AND THREE TRICKS

By the time Beem was approaching the city, his legs could barely carry him. He was hungry again. And what is there to eat on the side of the road? Nothing. Maybe a discarded watermelon rind, but that's not food. A dog like Beem needs meat, a good stew, borscht with bread (leftovers from the table)—in other words, everything that an ordinary man eats. And for the last two weeks, Beem had been on starvation rations. With his chest smashed by a heavy boot, not eating in this way was a slow death. If you add the fact that during his battle with the she-wolf, Beem had injured his crippled foot and was hobbling along on three legs, then you can imagine what he looked like when he entered his hometown.

But there are good people on this earth. At the very edge of town, he stopped near a tiny house with one window and one door. The house was surrounded by piles of brick, stone, lumber, and sacks of cement, and to one side there was half of a huge new house, without any windows or doors or a roof. The wind played in the windowframes, hissed in the brick piles, sang in the stacks of lumber, and howled in the upper stories —with a different voice in every section. There was nothing strange to Beem in this picture (there were construction sites everywhere), and, to be honest, he had often in his long travels turned to construction workers for something to eat. They understood his language and fed him. Once a joker in a crew poured a spoonful of vodka into a tin can and offered it to Beem, saying, "Here, pup, have a shot in honor of those who don't steal from us."

Beem had been insulted and turned away.

Everyone there laughed and called the joker Shurik. And that very same Shurik cut a big hunk of sausage—real, store-bought sausage, not from a garbage can—and gave it to Beem, "For telling the truth, Black Ear. Take it, you wise one."

And the men in the dirty coveralls laughed again. And Shurik added what must have been the funniest line of all: "You see, doggie, last night the air made our lumber shrink by another third."

And he laughed again, but without smiling.

Beem had his own interpretation of what Shurik had said: First of all, vodka was bad for a dog, and if you don't drink it, you get sausage; and second, all these men, smelling of brick, wood, and cement were good.

Remembering that, and guided by smells of the past, Beem lay down on the doorstep of the tiny house, the watchman's shed, too exhausted to move another step.

It was early morning. No one but the wind around. After a while someone coughed in the shed and began muttering to himself. Beem got up and scratched at the door. As usual, it opened. A man appeared at the door, bearded, one earflap of his cap down, one up, a raincoat pulled tightly over his sheepskin jacket. A man inspiring total trust in Beem.

"Ah, a visitor I see. Poor homeless thing, you've had a hard time. Well, come on in."

Beem entered the hut and lay down—no, fell—by the door.

166

The watchman cut off a piece of bread, soaked it in water, and gave it to Beem. He ate it gratefully and then put his head on his paws and looked at the old man.

And they talked about life.

The watchman was always lonely, no matter where he worked, and here was a living creature gazing at him with tender, human, exhausted, openly suffering, and thus amazing, eyes.

"Your life stinks, Black Ear, I can see that right off. Well, what is it? Hasn't your name come up on the waiting list for housing? Is that it? I'm in the same boat; turns come and go, but Mikhei is stuck. Think how many houses they've built, and I'm still moving around from site to site with this hut. If you was to run away, for instance, just try writing me a letter. There's no place to send it. I haven't had an address in five years. Just Mikhei, care of General Post Office. What kind of an address is that? An insult, that's what it is. Eat or drink—I've plenty of that. Clothing—I could even put on a tie and hat if I wanted to. But I have no place to live. What can you do! Temporary difficulties, they say. My name's Mikhei. I'm Mikhei," he said, pointing to his chest and sipping from a small bottle. (He sipped each time he got to the end of a sentence.)

Again Beem understood the monologue in his own way. That is, he heard the tone, the expression, the kindness and simplicity. Mikhei was a good man. Beem understood him and immediately fell into a light sleep, not really listening to the rest of the conversation. But still, out of respect for the man, he opened and closed his eyes, trying to overcome his sleepiness.

Mikhei went on in the same way. "You're asleep, and it's no problem. But I'm not allowed to. The inspector might come by. 'Where's Mikhei? Not here? Fire Mikhei. Right now.' That's the trouble. If you're not on duty, they come down on you. 'Where's

167

Mikhei? Not here? Fire him!' And that's that."

Through his doze, Beem heard only "Mikhei . . . Mikhei . . . Mikhei . . . and that's that."

Mikhei had a few more sips, wiped his mustache, salted a piece of bread, sniffed it and ate it, talking all the while. "And I'll tell you this, Black Ear, it's better to speak your piece to a dog. You don't get into trouble that way—the dog won't tell anyone, and you feel better. Now me, Mikhei, I'm a watchman. I have a gun. Now here's the question: What if there's more than one thief? What will Mikhei do? Nothing, that's what. And that's that. The law, they say. The law is fine—if you catch him, give 'im five years. Uh-huh! But you have to catch him, that's the rub. How are you going to do that? That's the problem. Now, you're a dog. Say I put twenty rabbits in a bag and let them all out at once, and I make you catch them. They'll run off in all directions—and that's that. So, you'll catch one. What about the rest? They'll all be gone!" Mikhei laughed so infectiously that Beem raised his head, to smile a bit.

But Beem was in no shape to smile.

The door opened. A man came in, another watchman, and said, "Relief. Go to sleep, Mikhei."

Mikhei went over to the bed and fell asleep immediately.

Relief sat in Mikhei's chair by the table and then noticed Beem.

"And who's this owl?" he asked, apparently noticing Beem's big eyes.

Beem sat up, as required by etiquette, and tiredly wagged his tail. ("I'm sick. I'm looking for my master.") Relief didn't understand a thing, the way many people don't understand dogs, and opened the door and kicked Beem out by way of answer. "Get lost, you mutt."

Beem left convinced that Relief was a lousy man. But he couldn't go any farther. The sop that Mikhei gave him made him feel even weaker, and sleep was knocking him off his feet.

168

Fighting it, Beem went into the house under construction, burrowed into pine-scented wood shavings, and again fell asleep.

No one bothered him all day. He slept until evening. In the twilight, he checked out the first floor of the house. He found half a loaf of bread on the windowsill, ate as much as he wanted, and buried the remaining piece in the soft ground near a trench. He did it all according to the rules; even when weak, you must obey the canine command: Bury a piece for a rainy day. Now he felt he could go on, and he went toward his own door.

Toward the door he had known from the first few days of his life, to the door behind which holy truth, pity, friendship, and compassion were so natural, so simple, that there was no point in naming concepts. And why should Beem even think about them? The door for which Beem was headed was part of his existence; it was his life. And that was that. No dog ever thinks that ordinary loyalty is anything special. But people have elevated this feeling dogs have into something unusual because not all people have a sense of loyalty and fidelity strong enough to be the root of their lives, the natural base of their existence.

The door for which Beem was headed was the door of his friend, and, therefore, also Beem's door. He was headed for the door of trust and life. Beem wanted to get to the door and either wait until his friend came or die. He no longer had the strength to search for him in town. He could only wait. Only wait.

But first Beem had to get past the Gray Man's neighborhood, and to do that he had to go past Tolik's house. And so it happened. Beem found himself by the gate to his friend's house and he couldn't, he simply couldn't walk by as though it were a stranger's. He lay down by the high brick wall, rolled up, and stuck his head out; a passerby would have thought he was wounded, or dying, or dead.

Beem certainly wouldn't go up to the door of that house. He would only rest by the fence for relief from his pain and sorrow,

169

and then he would go home. And perhaps, perhaps Tolik himself would appear. . . .

It was a dark evening.

A car drove up. It tore a piece of the wall from the darkness, then felt around the entire wall, and bugged its blinding eyes right at Beem. Beem looked up, his lids almost shut. The car purred and purred, and someone got out. The exhaust masked the smell of the man coming toward Beem, but when the car's eyes illuminated him, Beem sat up. Semyon Petrovich was coming toward him. He came up close, made sure it really was Beem and said, "He escaped. Well, imagine that!"

The other man got out, too (the one who drove Beem to Wolf Ravine before the storm), looked at the dog, and said in a kind voice, "He's a smart dog. He'll always get by."

Semyon Petrovich headed for Beem, unbuckling his belt.

"Beem, nice Beem. Here, boy. Come here, Beem."

Oh, no-o-o! Beem didn't believe him; Beem had lost his faith in that man, whatever good intentions he might have. Perhaps Semyon Petrovich was planning to return Beem to Tolik, realizing just how his son felt, but it was too late. Beem ran. He didn't walk; he ran from Semyon Petrovich along the fence illuminated by the car. Where did he get the strength?

Semyon Petrovich ran after him. The other man tried to cut Beem off, but Beem slipped into the darkness, crawled into a ditch, and then walked, barely dragging his feet. He went in the opposite direction from the one he had taken in the light.

And once more, Beem harkened to ancestral tricks: In a moment of danger, muddle your tracks! That's what rabbits, foxes, wolves, and other animals do. The fox and the wolf can actually backtrack so neatly that only an experienced hunter will be able to tell from the claw marks, after the fact, that he has been fooled. Trick number two is the loop—run off to the left, come back from the right—or the dodge (jump to the side from your backtrack). The third trick is to lie low; once you've confused

170

your trail, lie still in a hidden place and listen (if they go past, stay there, if they're coming straight for you, mix up the trail again). Real hunters know these three tricks well, but Semyon Petrovich had never been a hunter, even though he held a gun and went out every year on the opening day of the season.

So Semyon Petrovich ran in one direction, lighting the way with his flashlight, and Beem ran in the other, under cover of the ditch.

But the ditch came to an end—and Beem was up against a solid wall, an excavator scoop hanging over the top. He had trapped himself. He had gotten down into the ditch easily enough, but he couldn't climb out; there were walls on either side and in front. If he had been well and had all four legs, it would have been another matter, but now he could only walk out—not jump or leap out—only walk out.

Beem sat and sat, looked up at the scoop, managed to stand on one hind leg, leaning against the wall with his forepaws, examined the parapet, and sat down again. He seemed to be thinking, but he was simply listening—was the chase still on? Then he got up on the opposite wall, which didn't have a parapet, and saw the flashlight scurrying about in one spot, swinging from side to side, and then going out. He saw the car drive back, its side coming close to him. Beem huddled in the corner of the ditch and listened and quaked. The car drove past, very close.

Everything grew quiet. But there were sounds: weak carhorn blasts, the trolley bell—all familiar, harmless sounds.

A dog sat in a ditch on a cold, dark autumn night. And there was no one to help. And it had to leave, to get to its door. Beem tried jumping out, but he fell. And so he went back along his tracks, quietly, carefully, listening, and testing the walls. In one place he found a small landslide. He stood on it, got up on his good hind leg, and now he could reach the parapet. He began scooping the earth from the parapet into a mound under him; the more he worked, the higher the mound became. Beem took

171

breaks and worked some more. Finally he could lean his chest on the edge of the ditch, but there was no more dirt to pile up. He climbed down from his hill and rested. He wanted to howl, to call his master or Tolik, he wanted to howl desperately so that the whole city would hear! But he had to keep still—he had left a confused trail and was lying low. He got up resolutely, backed away from the mound he had created, and, forgetting his pain, threw his whole body upward, pushed against the mound with both hind legs, and fell on the very edge of the ditch, into the hollow he had earlier dug to rest in.

What helped him overcome such pain and weakness? Who knows? How can a wolf gnaw off his own foot when it's caught in a trap? We can only suppose that the wolf does it from an instinctive urge to be free, and that Beem forgot his own pain in his irrepressible urge to get to the door of kindness and trust.

Whatever the cause, Beem got out of the ditch and lay in the hollow on top.

The night was cold. The city was asleep, its stone and iron creaking even at night. Beem listened for a long time. Then, with a shudder, he went on.

On the way, he wandered into an open lobby, only because he absolutely had to rest, even for a short time—that's how weak he had grown. You can't lie in the street; you'll die (he had often seen dogs that had been run over). And it was cold on the pavement. In the lobby he huddled next to a hot radiator and slept.

A strange dog sleeping in the dark of night in a strange lobby.

15

AT THE FINAL DOOR AND THE SECRET OF THE IRON VAN

Beem woke up before dawn. He didn't want to leave the warm, hospitable spot where no one had disturbed his sleep. He felt a little stronger, and he tried to stand, but he couldn't right away. So he sat. That worked, but it made him dizzy (just the way he felt after the kick in the chest). The walls lurched to one side, the banisters of the staircase quivered, and the steps blended into a mountain and then crumpled up like an accordion, and the light fixture swayed along with the ceiling. Beem sat and waited to see what would happen next, sat with his head down.

The dizziness stopped as abruptly as it had begun. Beem crawled down the steps on his stomach. The door was open, and he crawled out, lay in the refreshing cold, and then stood. He was on the brink of losing consciousness, and therefore he felt no pain; he went on, reeling, obeying an invisible force.

He surely wouldn't have made it to his door if he hadn't come across a garbage pail and a little dog that was rummaging in it. Beem sat nearby. The dog, long-haired and unkempt, sniffed him and wagged her tail.

"Where are you going?" she asked. It was Shaggy.

Beem recognized her immediately—they had met in the

fields that long-ago day, when she had been eating the roots of bulrushes. And so he replied trustingly and sadly, with his eyes, "I'm very sick, my friend."

The dog returned to the garbage can and, by turning her head toward Beem and wagging her tail, invited her guest to join her.

And, with a little bit of this and that, a crust here, a fish head there, Beem had a filling meal. His strength returned slowly, and soon, licking his chops and thanking Shaggy, he went on, feeling more solid.

A garbage can at a difficult moment in your life can be a wonderful thing! From that moment on, Beem would have had respect for such places, if only . . .

In the gray, predawn light, when the remnants of yesterday's smog had settled in a translucent gray haze, Beem finally reached his house. There it was! There was the window from which he and Ivan Ivanovich sometimes watched the sun rise. Would he be looking out now? Beem sat across the street and watched, watched with joy and hope. He felt good. He crossed the street, without rushing, but with his head up, smiling, as though about to meet his friend any second. It was a moment of anticipating happiness. What living creature isn't happier in anticipation than at the actual instant of happiness?

And so, in the middle of the street, in front of his own house, not far from his door, Beem was happy in the hope that had arisen anew.

But suddenly he saw a terrible sight: that woman came out! Beem sat down, his eyes wide open in fear and his body trembling. She threw a brick at him. Beem went back across the street.

There was no one on the street that early, not even the janitors with their brooms. The woman and Beem looked at each other. She had obviously decided to stand and not let him pass; she planted her feet more firmly and stood in the archway, fists firmly placed on hips. She looked at Beem haughtily, contemptuously, triumphantly, proudly, with a sense of her personal worth, superiority, and rightness. Beem was helpless, but he still had his dependable teeth, which were terrible in a predeath bite. He knew it, he hadn't forgotten, and so he crouched and lifted his upper lip, baring his front teeth. The person and the dog looked at each other fixedly. The minutes seemed long to Beem.

As for the woman, we know something about her from her previous encounters with Beem. She was a totally free woman —free of capitalist exploitation, free of any remote concept of her duty toward socialism, untrammeled by labor. But she was still a slave to her stomach, even though she wasn't conscious of that fact. And she did have her responsibilities. She rose before dawn, long before any of the other residents of the large building. Her most important responsibility, in her eyes, was to see what strangers left which apartment at dawn; whose lights were still burning when everyone else was asleep; who went out fishing or hunting, and with whom; and who was the first to bring out their garbage. Then she would check to see what was thrown out and figure out its meaning—bottles meant that he was hiding them from his wife; a junky old coat meant that the cheapskate had been saving a useless old rag; rotten meat meant that she was incapable of managing a household; and so on. And if a girl were to come home at dawn, then the woman was at the peak of her glory. She hated dogs and their owners, and observing them was therefore one of the most important of her duties, and she hurled various rarely used words after them—her supply was vast, proof of her great memory and erudition.

All this was essential for her daily exchange of news with several other free women when they got together on the benches; no one was forgotten, and nothing was forgiven. A talent! She issued an unpublished bulletin daily. That was her

175

second duty to society. It even included international news (she heard it herself—war was coming, so hoard grain and salt; and the rumor spread, thanks to other, like-minded old women, who added a more official-sounding source, an assistant professor who "should know").

And, as we already know, she called herself "a Soviet woman," no less, and prided herself on it. What a monster a child of hers would have been!

She had two days off a week. Sundays she bought things at the market from kolkhoz farmers, and Mondays she sold them. Thus, without having chickens, or a garden, or fishing nets, she sold eggs, chickens, tomatoes, and fresh fish and everything else people needed. And thanks to her third duty (her activities on her days off!), she had a bankbook and lived well, which is why she never had a job. She lived in an apartment decorated in accordance with her high cultural state (two sideboards, three mirrors, a cheap print of *The Girl and the Swan,* a big plaster eagle, plastic flowers, a refrigerator, a TV). She had everything you were supposed to have and nothing that you weren't.

And she stood in the middle of the archway, and Beem couldn't get past her. He should have left, gone away, but he was in no condition to leave his own house. He was going to wait with teeth bared until his enemy left, wait as long as it took. He could outwait her!

But a lone van appeared in the gray haze and stopped between the woman and Beem. The van was dark gray with metal over the windows. Two men got out and approached the woman. Beem watched attentively without budging.

"Who's dog is that?" asked a man with a mustache, pointing at Beem.

"Mine," the woman replied nastily.

"Why don't you get it off the street?" the second man, much younger, asked.

"Just try it. You see the piece of rope on its neck—it bit right

176

through the rope. The stupid thing has rabies. I'm sure of it."

"Tie it up. We'll take it away."

"I reported it. And I went down and I asked them to take it away. Nothing! Just a bunch of bureaucrats! They're driving me crazy, these bureaucrats!" She was shouting.

"Come on," said the one with the mustache.

The younger man got a pistol out of the van and the other one got a net from the side of the van, a net for catching butterflies the size of sheep. The man with the gun went first, and the other one followed, net ready.

Beem saw the gun. He wagged his tail as if to say, "A gun! A gun! I know guns!"

"He's being friendly," the young man said. "He's not rabid. Look!"

The man with the mustache came forward. Beem could tell that he smelled of dogs.

"Well, of course, you're good people!" Beem said with his manner.

But a dog's whimper, hopeless and bitter, came from the van. Beem understood everything—it was a ruse! Even the gun was a ruse. It was all a ruse! He jumped aside but—too late. The hoop of the net covered him. Beem jumped up and found himself in the net; he had pulled it over the hoop himself.

Beem bit the ropes, snarled, and fought frantically, violently, as if in a fit. But he exhausted his last ounce of strength quickly and quieted down. The dogcatchers put the net through the door of the van and shook Beem onto the floor.

The door slammed shut.

The man with the mustache turned to the woman, who was smug and happy. "What are you smiling about? If you don't know how to keep dogs, then don't. Don't torture them. You've stuffed your stupid frog face, but your dog is starved to death —it doesn't even look like a dog anymore."

(He was quite observant. The lowered corners of her fat

177

mouth, the flat nose, and the bulging eyes really made the woman look like a frog.)

"How dare you insult me, a Soviet woman, you lousy, mangy dogcatcher!" And she went on hurling abuse at him, not shy about the words she chose.

"You watch yourself!" the man shouted at her. "Or I'll catch you in the net and throw you in the iron box. People like you should be shut up in there at least one week out of the year." And he took a few steps toward her with the net.

The woman ran indoors to write a complaint against him. She wrote directly to the chairman of the town council, berating him as much as she had the dogcatchers.

The sun was rising, big and yellow, cold and dreary. It avoided the morning haze, and in places the grayish fog floated over the city like a ragged veil. Some blocks were sunny; some weren't.

The dark-gray, iron-cold van drove out of town and turned into the yard of a solitary house, surrounded by a high fence. There was a sign over the entrance: "No Admittance Without Authorization—Danger." This was the dog pound's quarantine station, where rabid dogs were burned to ashes. Stray dogs were brought here, too, as possible carriers of epidemics—they weren't burned but were skinned or sent to be used in scientific experiments. Other animals with infectious diseases were treated here if they merited it; horses, for instance, were given medication until the last minute of their lives and were destroyed only if they were suffering from glanders. The disease is rarely seen nowadays, because there are so few horses.

The two men who had caught Beem were ordinary workers here. And they weren't bad men, either. They were always in danger of catching some disease or other or being bitten by a mad dog. They cleared the city of strays or picked up dogs at the owners' request. They considered that part of their work unpleasant and painful, though they received a bonus for every dog they caught.

Beem didn't hear the van pull up into the yard and the two men get out. He was unconscious.

He came to several hours later. Shaggy, his old friend, was sitting next to him. She was licking Beem's nose and ears.

What an amazing creature a dog is! If a pup dies, the mother will lick its nose, lick its ears, lick and lick endlessly, massaging its tummy. And sometimes the puppy revives. For dogs in general, massage is part of the care of newborns.

Shaggy was licking Beem for reasons we don't understand. She had obviously seen a lot in her lifetime, and perhaps this wasn't her first trip here. Who knows?

A thin ray of light peeped through the door and fell on Beem. He raised his head. They were alone in the iron prison, Beem and Shaggy. Overcoming the pain in his chest, he tried to shift, to change his position, but his attempt failed. The second time, he tucked all his feet under him, getting his side away from the cold metal. Shaggy, also chilled to the bone, cuddled up to him. It was a little warmer together.

Two dogs, lying in an iron prison, awaited their fate.

Beem kept looking at the door, at the thin ray of sunlight, the only sign of the outside world. In the distance, he heard a shot. Beem started. Oh, how well he knew the sound! It reminded him of his master, Ivan Ivanovich; it was hunting, it was the forest, it was freedom, and it was the way you called your dog if it was lost or too engrossed in the trail of a bird or hare. Where did Beem get the strength to get up and stagger to the door, to press his nose against the crack and breathe in the air of freedom? But he was on his feet, he was resurrected. And he began pacing slowly from one end of the van to the other. Then he went back to the door, sniffing some more. He realized that something upsetting was going on in the yard. And he paced

179

and paced some more, his claws clicking on the iron floor, un-kinking his muscles, preparing for something.

It's hard to say how much time passed. But Beem started scratching at the door.

This door in no way resembled the others Beem had known. It was covered with iron; there were jagged, rusty tears in it. But it was a door, now the only door through which he could call for help and sympathy.

Night came. Cold and frosty.

Shaggy began howling.

Beem went on scratching. He chewed at the pieces of iron and scratched some more, lying down now. He called. He begged.

By morning no noise was coming from the van. Shaggy had stopped howling, and Beem was quiet, too. Once in a while he gave a feeble scratch. Whether he was exhausted or whether he had resigned himself to his fate, having lost all hope, who knows? It was the secret of the iron van.

16

ENCOUNTERS DURING THE SEARCH, TRACES OF BEEM ON EARTH, AND FOUR SHOTS

There are more people in town on Sundays than during the week; they walk, eat, run, buy, sell, crowd into trains, buses, and trolleys like sardines. By midday, the crowd thins out a bit and regroups in the evening; some are returning from the villages and forests, and some are returning to the villages and forests.

And so it was no surprise that on one Sunday, Khrisan Andreyevich and Alyosha came to town. They had decided that Alyosha would try to find Blackie while his father sold their produce at the market. Khrisan Andreyevich had let Alyosha roam the city before, without worrying about him (the boy knew the number of the trolley, he knew his bus stop, and he certainly would never get into trouble). Usually Alyosha was given three rubles to buy whatever he wanted or to go wherever he wanted, including the movies or the circus. This time Khrisan Andreyevich stuffed fifteen rubles in the boy's pocket and said, "If you should come across Blackie and they won't give him up, offer them ten. If they don't agree, go up to twelve. If they still say no, give them fifteen. And if they still don't want to, write down the address and come to me—I'll go see them myself. Don't stay out late. I want to get on the bus by four; the days are getting shorter, and I don't like traveling in the dark. And be courteous when you ask about Blackie: 'May I ask you something, comrade?' And then go into the facts: 'We're from the country, shepherds, and we can't manage without a dog, and ours is missing. It ran away to the city.' There are a lot of kind people, you know. Just ask around."

A sturdy, solemn boy walked through the city, occasionally stopping people who looked trustworthy to him.

"May I ask you something, comrade? We're shepherds, you see, and. . . ."

He saw an unbelievable number of fat people, particularly women, but he let them pass (they obviously didn't work and that's why they were so fat). But it was a fat comrade who heard the boy asking someone else and stopped to suggest that he go to the railroad station (every young person in town will pass through there in a day—one of them will surely know something). Alyosha asked every kid he saw.

Meanwhile Tolik, too, had left his house to go looking for Beem. He had been searching persistently for three days, after school, and he decided to spend the whole day today. It was Sunday, no school.

A clean boy from a cultured family was walking through the city, looking into people's faces, seeming to study the passersby, and asking, "Mister, tell me, please, have you seen a dog with a black ear? White with tan markings? No, you haven't? Too bad. Forgive me."

Tolik had already been to Stepanovna's, despite his parents' ban, had already given Lusya the Czech pencils that can't be bought in any store, had already told them that Beem had spent the night at his house and then disappeared; he learned from Stepanovna that Ivan Ivanovich, whom he had never set eyes on, had written that he was coming home soon. Tolik planned to drop by this evening—maybe there would be news of Beem, and anyway, Lusya promised to give him a picture she was doing, called "Our Beem."

On a street near the station, a tanned, healthy-looking boy of thirteen, wearing a grown-up suit, stopped him and asked, "May I ask you a question, comrade?"

Tolik liked being treated like an adult. "Of course." And then he added, "What would you like?"

"We're shepherds. And our dog has run off into town. Perhaps you've seen it? It's white with tan markings and has a solid black ear. And one leg is black, too—"

"What's the dog's name?" Tolik shouted.

"Blackie," Alyosha said.

"It's Beem!"

The boys filled each other in. Tolik found out how and when Beem had been bought and when he had left the village; Alyosha learned that it was Blackie who had gone to Tolik's house, and no other dog. It all fit. Beem was somewhere in the city. Neither boy thought about who would keep him once he was found. The important thing was to find him, and fast.

"Let's go by the railroad station first," Alyosha suggested. "A man told me to do that."

"There's loads of people; one of them must have seen Beem."

The idea was very naive, but neither Tolik nor Alyosha was aware of it. They felt the spirit of camaraderie and were united by a single desire—their love for Beem. And they even imagined that they might just possibly run across Beem himself.

"And then we'll go see your Stepanovna," Alyosha decided. "He's bound to go there, too. In fact, that's where he's going. He's headed for home."

"We'll go there, too."

Tolik liked Alyosha's seriousness and simplicity. Meetings like this lead to lifelong friendships. They had already questioned over a hundred people, and they went on picking out likely candidates.

That morning a gray-haired man, leaning on a cane, stepped out of the express train and joined the general bustle in the station. He stopped outside and looked around. He was like a man who had been gone for a long time and was checking to see that everything was still the same—to see if anything had changed. Just then, two strange boys came up to him. One of them, obviously from the country, spoke.

"May I ask you a question, comrade?"

The gray-haired man, cocking his head to one side and hiding a smile, replied, "Of course you may, comrade."

The other boy, obviously from the city, continued, "Tell us please, have you seen a dog with a black ear, white with tan—"

The man grabbed the boy's shoulder and cried out with undisguised concern, "Beem?"

"Yes, Beem. Have you seen him? Where?"

The three of them sat down on a bench in the park by the station. And all three trusted one another without any hesitation, even though the boys didn't know the man and didn't know he was Ivan Ivanovich, Beem's master, and wouldn't have guessed it readily if he hadn't told them.

His friends wouldn't have recognized him readily, either. He had become slightly stooped, his face was thinner, and he had more wrinkles (an operation near the heart is no picnic); but his eyes were the same—attentive, penetrating, seeming to see right into a person's heart. The dark-brown eyes were the only indication that the man had had brown hair. Now his hair was white as snow.

Tolik told him everything he knew about Beem, including the fact that he was lame and sick. Alyosha told them all about his life in the village. The boys liked everything about Ivan Ivanovich. He talked to them as if they were adults, sometimes resting his hand on the shoulder of whichever boy was speaking, and he listened without interrupting, and he had such white hair, and they liked his name, and, most important, he liked them, boys whom he had never met before—that was very clear. That's why he said, "You're good boys. Let's be friends, real friends. And now, let's go to my house. Judging by everything you've said, Beem must be there by now."

On the way, he found out about their families, where they lived, what they did, and what they liked.

"You herd sheep—that's good, Alyosha. And you go to school? It must be hard."

"You have to know how to feed sheep," Alyosha replied, as his father often did. "It's hard work. Getting the sheep to spread out in front without trampling the grass—it's no joke. You run yourself ragged; your legs ache. And you have to get up at the crack of dawn. And there's lots to worry about. It's easier with a dog—it's more help than a man who doesn't know a fig about the work. And we really can't manage without a dog. We're shepherds. What can you do?"

"And you, Tolik, what do you do?"

"Me?" Tolik asked in surprise. "I go to school."

"What kind of animals do you have at home?" Alyosha asked.

"None. I used to have guinea pigs, but my mother made me get rid of them. She said they smelled."

"You come visit me; I'll show you ours. Our cow Milka is worth her weight in gold—you can climb under her belly and she won't kick. And she licks your cap and hands. And our rooster is the best; they call that kind a leader—he crows first and the others follow. There aren't many like that around. But we don't have a dog. We had one, but it died. We had Blackie, but he ran off." Alyosha sighed. "Too bad, he was so nice."

Ivan Ivanovich rang Stepanovna's doorbell. She came out with Lusya.

"Oh, Ivan Ivanovich! What will I do now? Beem's gone. He was at Tolik's house three days ago, but he didn't come home."

"He didn't—" Ivan Ivanovich grew thoughtful. But, to cheer up the boys, he said, "We'll find him, we certainly will."

185

Stepanovna gave him the keys to his apartment, and all five of them went there. The room was just as he had left it: the same wall of books, which amazed Alyosha, and the same desk, and it was even cleaner (Stepanovna's efforts, of course), but it was so empty—Beem wasn't there. The plain piece of paper was on his bed—Ivan Ivanovich's letter. Stepanovna had saved it. Ivan Ivanovich turned his back to his guests and looked out the window, depressed. Stepanovna thought that she heard him moan.

"You should have a rest after your trip, Ivan Ivanovich," she suggested.

He lay down on the bed, staring up at the ceiling, while they stood around in silence. Stepanovna tried to talk his pain away.

"So, the operation was a success? If they let you travel alone, it must have been."

"Everything's fine, Stepanovna, fine. Thank you, dear woman, for everything. Everyone should treat his family the way you treat strangers."

"Come now! Don't be silly! What stuff and nonsense you're prattling. Everyone should help a neighbor. Things should always be kind and good." (Stepanovna was embarrassed when she was praised.)

A few minutes later, Ivan Ivanovich got up and looked at the boys.

"Here's the plan. You look for him here, in the neighborhood, ask around—he has to be nearby. And I—" He thought for a bit. "I'll go to a place—maybe he's fallen in with guard dogs— somewhere."

As they were leaving, Lusya gave Tolik a drawing, "Our Beem." Tolik showed it to Alyosha.

"You did that yourself?"

"Yes."

"Are you a painter?" Alyosha asked.

"No," Lusya laughed. "I just got promoted to fifth grade."

186

Beem's likeness was very good: the black ear, black leg, the tan spots, and the big eyes; one ear might have been a bit too long, but that wasn't important.

So Alyosha and Tolik set out on the search again. They chose people by their faces (after a consultation) and asked the same question and gave a description of Beem.

Ivan Ivanovich, while still resting on the bed, had decided he had to get over to the quarantine station immediately! To warn the dogcatchers about Beem, to describe him, to give them money to let him know if they found Beem. Maybe Beem was already there. He left Tolik's place three days ago. Hurry, hurry!

He took a cab and soon found himself at the gates of the station. There was no one there but the watchman (it was Sunday). But he answered Ivan Ivanovich's questions readily and at length.

"They didn't catch any dogs on Thursday and Friday, and yesterday's are in the van. No one knows how many there are in there. The vet will be here tomorrow to decide which ones go to science, which ones get a shot and are skinned—some are buried with their skins on. That's what the vets are for. And some are just burned, you know."

"Do you ever get hunting dogs?" Ivan Ivanovich said.

"Not often. They don't put those to sleep and don't turn them over for experiments, either. First they wait for the owners to call for them, or they call the Hunting Society—to see if they can find out anything. That's what the vets are for. One of the guys said that there's a hunting dog in there—a white one, in terrible shape. The woman who owned it turned it in herself. Maybe her husband died."

Is it Beem? Ivan Ivanovich thought. "Please let me see the van. I'm looking for my dog; it's a marvelous dog. Maybe it's in there. Please."

The watchman wouldn't hear of it.

"There are no marvelous dogs in there. Just diseased ones to

187

keep them from spreading it." He was determined. His face had changed. He thrust out his chin and waved the man away from the gates. Ivan Ivanovich was stunned and weak, unable to do anything. The watchman couldn't resist taking advantage of his superior position, and he added, "See the sign? 'No Admittance.'"

Ivan Ivanovich had lost all hope of getting inside, but he tried, anyway.

"What kind of man are you! I had a tough operation. I've had shrapnel near my heart since the war. I came home, and my dog was gone."

"What? You had shrapnel in you for over twenty years? Right there?" The watchman was himself again. "Just think! That's hard to believe. My goodness." And he invited Ivan Ivanovich in, opening the latch. "Come in. But don't tell anyone."

Ivan Ivanovich let the cab go, hoping he would take Beem home on a leash, and went over to the van. He was walking with great hope. If Beem was there, then he would see him right away and caress him, and if he wasn't, that meant Beem was alive and he'd find him.

"Beem, my Beem. My boy, my silly Beem," he whispered to himself as he walked.

And the watchman opened the van door.

Ivan Ivanovich reeled in horror.

Beem lay with his nose toward the door. His lips and gums were torn by the jagged, rusty edges of the iron. The claws of his forepaws were bloody.

He had scratched at his final door for a long time. He had scratched until his last breath. And how little he had been asking—freedom and trust, that was all.

Shaggy, cowering in a corner, howled.

Ivan Ivanovich put his hand on Beem's head—his faithful, loyal, loving friend.

It began to snow. Two snowflakes fell on Beem's nose—and they did not melt.

Meanwhile, Alyosha and Tolik, even closer friends now, were walking around town. They asked and asked, and finally ended up at the veterinary station where Tolik had once taken Beem. There they learned that there were no dogs there and that if a dog was missing the place to look was the quarantine station at the pound, because that's where the dogcatchers worked.

Our two boys were not the helpless sort who send letters addressed merely "To Grandpa in the Country," and less than an hour later they were hurrying from the bus stop to the pound.

Ivan Ivanovich was just coming out. When he saw them, he hurried over and asked, "You here, too?"

"They told us to," Alyosha said.

"Is Beem here?" Tolik asked.

Silence.

"Was he here?" Alyosha asked again.

"No, boys. Beem wasn't here." Ivan Ivanovich was trying to hide his sorrow and pain; it was very difficult to do in his condition.

And Tolik, raising his thick black eyebrows and pursing his lips, said, "Ivan Ivanovich—don't fool us—please."

"Beem isn't here, boys," Ivan Ivanovich repeated more firmly and confidently. "We have to look for him. Search for him."

The snow came down in a fine powder.

Quiet snow.

White snow.

Cold snow, which fell and covered the earth until the next cycle, the new beginning of life, until spring.

The man with hair as white as snow walked in the empty lot.

189

Two boys, holding his hand, walked next to him, ready to look for their common friend. And they were full of hope.

A lie can be as holy as the truth. A dying man smiles and tells his loved ones, "I feel much better." A mother sings to her hopelessly ill child and smiles.

And life goes on. It goes on because there is hope.

The boys went on looking for Beem all day. And in the evening, at dusk, Tolik saw Alyosha off at "our" bus stop.

"And this is my papa," Alyosha said.

Khrisan Andreyevich shook hands.

"I see you made a friend. When will you come visit Alyosha? You're always welcome."

Alyosha replied for Tolik.

"He'll come soon. And I'll come to see Ivan Ivanovich. We're going to look some more."

"Fine. Good. Tell me all of this on the way home. Look. Our bus is coming."

Alyosha gave his father the fifteen rubles. "It's all there. I didn't need it."

"I see," Papa said sadly.

Tolik waved at the bus. He was sorry to part with his new friend and happy that he existed. Now Tolik could live in anticipation of his meetings with Alyosha. And it was Beem who had left that trace on earth.

At home, Tolik told his papa confidently, "Beem is somewhere in town. And we'll find him. We will."

"Who's we?"

"Alyosha, Ivan Ivanovich, and me. We'll find him, you'll see."

"Who's Alyosha? Who's Ivan Ivanovich?" his mama asked.

"Alyosha is a boy from the country, his father is Uncle Khrisan, and Ivan Ivanovich is—I don't know who he is—he's kind and good—he's Beem's master."

190

"Then why are you looking for Beem if his master is here?" Papa asked.

Tolik couldn't answer; he didn't even understand the question because it was so unexpected and so complex.

"I don't know."

And late that night, when Tolik was asleep and dreaming about Alyosha's cow licking his hat, his parents were arguing in the next room.

"Your son is growing up without any supervision," Papa said sternly.

"And where are you?"

"I'm at work."

"And I work, too. You leave the house and that's fine for you. And I—well, just cleaning the house takes all my energy."

"No matter where you work, or who you are, there are responsibilities that have to be taken care of. I'm talking about something else—who's going to bring up Tolik? You or me? Or both of us? In that case we have to speak the same language."

"Probably neither you or me."

"Then who?"

"Our only hope lies in the school," Mama said, trying to make peace.

"And the street?"

"Even the street. All kinds of children play outside."

"And who's going to instill in him a sense of honesty, I ask you?" Papa had raised his voice again.

"Here, read this. No, I'll read it to you. Listen." Mama read from the newspaper, picking out phrases from the article: " 'Organization, vigilant supervision, strict accountability, deep interest—that's what develops honesty in people' . . . 'The honest man must be lauded, raised on shields.' Hear that? on shields! Mama threw herself face down on the sofa.

191

Papa did not want to continue the argument because he loved Mama, and she loved him, and he was always the first to make up. And they never had long arguments, anyway. And so this time, too, he said soothingly, "Well, we'll just have to figure this out. I'll try to find Beem. I'll try. His master is back, so Tolik won't be dragging the dog here, and if we were to find the dog, it would only increase our authority in his eyes."

But those weren't at all the words that were going through his mind. That evening, Semyon Petrovich was neither calm nor confident. His son was growing up and beyond him, and he, Tolik's own father, had had nothing to do with it, he hadn't even noticed. Semyon Petrovich was thinking. And he remembered a young teenager he had seen outside a beer hall on the river-front. The boy was leaning against a wall, reeling and stumbling, and shouting, and weeping inconsolably. The memory made him shudder. Semyon Petrovich pictured Tolik in front of that beer hall five years from now, and cringed. He sat down next to his wife and asked in a soft, placating voice, which surprised her, "Maybe we could buy Tolik a good dog? Or get Beem's master to let him have Beem? We'll pay well. What do you think?"

"Oh, I don't know, Semyon, I don't know. Let's buy one, I guess."

Semyon Petrovich had forgotten one little thing: that friendship and trust can't be bought or sold. He didn't know that he couldn't find Beem, even if he had really wanted to. Yet Beem, our Beem, had left his mark on Tolik's father. That night, Beem worried Semyon Petrovich, too.

Beem was still in the iron van that night. In the morning, Tolik's father would organize a search for him. Would Semyon Petrovich find him, would he uncover the secret of the iron van, would he ever comprehend the full force of Beem's striving toward light, toward freedom, friendship, and trust?

No, it wouldn't happen, and for the simplest of reasons. The

192

next morning, Monday, Ivan Ivanovich took his gun and went to the pound. He met the two dogcatchers, and learned with terrible pain and bitterness that they had taken Beem right in front of his house. Now they were incensed by the woman's behavior and cursed her roundly. It was hard on Ivan Ivanovich to learn that Beem had been the victim of treachery and lies. He did not blame the two workers who had done their job, even though the younger fellow obviously felt guilty, if only because he had believed the woman.

"If I had only known—" He didn't finish, and struck his fist on the van. "That's what I get for believing a viper like that."

Ivan Ivanovich asked them to drive him and Beem to the forest, and offered them five rubles. They agreed readily. The three men rode in the cab of the van.

In the clearing where Ivan Ivanovich used to sit before hunting and listen to the forest, in the clearing where Beem had rubbed his face in the fallen leaves in misery and anticipation, a few feet away from the stump, they buried Beem. And they covered his grave lightly with a thin layer of yellowed leaves mixed with snow.

The forest rustled steadily and softly.

Ivan Ivanovich unsheathed his gun, loaded it, and, after a moment's thought, shot into the air.

The forest echoed the shot sadly, without a ripple, autumnally. It died off in the distance with a short moan.

And the master shot again. And waited for the forest to moan.

The dogcatchers stared at Ivan Ivanovich in amazement. But he didn't move. He reloaded the gun and shot twice more, slowly, waiting after each shot for the echo to die. Then he put the gun away and walked over to the stump.

The older man asked, "Why did you do that—shoot four times?"

"That's the custom. One shot for each year the dog lived. Beem was four. Any hunter in hearing distance takes off his hat and stands for a minute in silence."

"Get that!" the younger man said. "Just like a scene in a tragedy." He went back to the van, got in, and shut the door.

Ivan Ivanovich sat down on the stump.

The forest murmured monotonously, almost in its winter voice, with a cold, naked, uncozy sound. There wasn't much snow. It was time, but the snow was late. Perhaps that's why the forest sounded grumpy, sleepy, and so hopeless, as if winter would never come and there would never be another spring.

And suddenly, in the emptiness that was left after the loss of his only friend, Ivan Ivanovich felt a warmth. He didn't guess right off what it was, but it was the two boys Beem had brought to him without knowing it. And they would come back, more than once.

Ivan Ivanovich seemed very, very strange to the simple dog-catchers when he climbed into the van, saying to himself, "It's not true. Spring will come. And there will be crocuses again. Russia has its winters and its springs. That's what our Russia is like—it has winters and it has springs."

On the way back, the young dogcatcher suddenly stopped the van beside a small village near the highway, opened the van, and let out Shaggy.

"I won't go on. I don't want to!" he shouted. "Run to the village, dog, save yourself. You'll be all right there."

"What's the matter with you? They know there were two dogs!" the older man shouted.

"One died, and the other ran away. That's all. I don't want to do this anymore. That's all."

Shaggy ran away from the road and sat and watched the van drive off. Then she ran into the village, ran to be with people. A sensible dog.

Ivan Ivanovich had learned back in the forest that the young dogcatcher was named Ivan, and so was the older one. They were three Ivans, an unusual coincidence. That brought them closer together, and they parted as friends. And yet there was really only one thing they shared—they had buried a dog that couldn't stand imprisonment. Sometimes people are brought together by major events, and then they go their separate ways, and sometimes people are brought together by small things and remain friends forever.

When Ivan Ivanovich got out of the van, he offered the promised five rubles to young Ivan, who pushed his hand away.

"I don't want to anymore. I won't. That's all!"

It became perfectly clear that he blamed himself for Beem's death; he felt the reproach of the dead. That's the most horrible kind of reproach, because the dead can't forgive or feel any compassion or pity for the repentant sinner. Young Ivan had taken his mistake utterly to heart. And that did him honor, and was yet another trace of kind, loyal, and faithful Beem. But the older Ivan didn't feel any spiritual discomfort—he took the money from Ivan Ivanovich's hand and put it in his back pocket —gratefully. And he wasn't to blame; he was taking the payment they had agreed on for his work. And as for catching Beem, he had only been doing his job.

That day, Semyon Petrovich organized a search. First of all, the following advertisement appeared in the paper: "Missing: a setter, white with a black ear, answers to Beem, a well-trained dog of exceptional intelligence. Generous reward for information as to its whereabouts." With his address, of course.

The big city was abuzz about Beem. Telephones rang persistently; sympathetic letters poured in; scouts raced around the city looking for him.

And so Beem was twice-renowned—once, when he was alive, he had been branded mad; and the second time, after his death, he was called "exceptionally intelligent." Semyon Petrovich was responsible for Beem's final fame.

But there were no traces of Beem, even though they

searched throughout the winter and beyond. Who could have known? Young Ivan quit his job, and for obvious reasons did not answer the ad; the older Ivan had been warned by Ivan Ivanovich not to say a word. And there was no one else in the whole world who knew that Beem was buried in the forest, in the recently frozen ground, dusted with snow, and that no one would ever see him again.

The winter that year was a harsh one, with two black blizzards. The white snow in the fields turned black. But our familiar clearing stayed pure and white. It was protected by the forest.

17

THE FOREST SIGHS
(Instead of an Epilogue)

And once more spring came. The sun was pushing winter away. It hobbled off, melting, on soggy, weak legs, and right behind it came more and more warm days, tearing the snows apart into dirty gray clumps. Spring is always ruthless with dying winter.

And the streams calmed down, no longer hurrying, smaller and smaller, thinner and thinner, almost stopping at night. The spring was late and steady.

"Such a spring means a good harvest," Khrisan Andreyevich said one night when he and Alyosha slept over at Ivan Ivanovich's.

Soon they would be taking the sheep out to pasture, but during the school term Alyosha would only help his father bring them out in the morning and bring them back at night.

Alyosha came to visit alone a few times, too. On such days he and Tolik were inseparable and they looked for Beem. But once, when they were all having tea at Ivan Ivanovich's, Khrisan Andreyevich said, "If no one's answered the ad in the paper, it must mean that someone has taken Beem far, far away. Russia's a big place, boys. You won't find him. If he had died, then someone would certainly have answered the ad to say where, and that they had seen the dog, and claim the reward.

The important thing is that he's alive. You can't find every dog you lose. And there's nothing you can do about it, really." He exchanged a knowing look with Ivan Ivanovich and added, "So, there's no point in looking for him anymore. Am I right, Ivan Ivanovich?"

Ivan Ivanovich nodded.

The search ended that day. Only the memory was left, and it remained all their lives, until their dying days. Maybe, many years later, they told their children about Beem.

When they left, Khrisan Andreyevich carried a month-old sheep dog inside his coat—a gift from Ivan Ivanovich. Alyosha was ecstatic.

Another new puppy was playing with an old shoe in Ivan Ivanovich's room. Another Beem—with a pedigree and the typical markings of an English setter. Ivan Ivanovich had bought this one for Tolik and himself.

But he would never forget his old friend. He would never forget the hunting dawns Beem had given him, or his kindness and all-forgiving friendship. The memory of his faithful friend and of Beem's sad fate disturbed the old man. That's why he was back in the old clearing, seated on the old stump. He looked around. He had come to listen to the forest.

It was an unbelievably quiet spring day.

The sky had sprinkled the field thickly with crocuses. This miracle had happened many times in Ivan Ivanovich's life. And here it was again, quiet but powerful in its true simplicity, and amazing in its inimitable newness. The birth of life—spring.

The forest was silent, just barely awakening from its long sleep, sprinkled by heaven, and disturbed by the warm sunspots that played on the shiny, marvelously delicate tongues of the unfurled buds. Ivan Ivanovich felt that he was sitting in a magnificent temple with a blue floor, a blue cupola, and columns of living oaks. It was like a dream.

But suddenly—what could it mean? A brief sound rippled through the forest—a deep sigh. It was very much like a sigh of relief that after a long wait the trees were coming to life once more, their buds starting to open. Otherwise, why had the branches stirred, and why did the titmouse twitter, and the woodpecker drum a tattoo, calling his beloved, filling the forest with his love call? He was one of the first, like the woodcock, to signal the majestic symphony of spring; but the woodcock calls softly in the twilight, cautiously: "Gor, gor, gor!"—which means "Gorgeous!" And the woodpecker finds a hollow tree trunk and proudly, boldly, and persistently proclaims on his primitive instrument: "P-p-p-p-perfect!"

It was clear: the forest had sighed in relief because the miracle had begun and the time had come for fulfilling hope. And the birds were responding to their savior. Ivan Ivanovich heard it all. That's why he had come, to listen to the forest and its creatures.

And he would have been happy, as he was every year at this time, if there hadn't been a patch of land on the edge of the clearing—a patch that wasn't strewn with crocuses, but covered by fresh dirt mixed with last year's fallen leaves. It was sad to look upon a patch like that in springtime, particularly at the very start of the swelling chorus of joy.

But the new, tiny Beem was looking up at Ivan Ivanovich with his kind, naive, gentle, and innocent eyes. He had already won over Tolik; he had begun his life with kindness, this tiny Beem.

What will his fate be? thought Ivan Ivanovich. Please don't let this new Beem, beginning life, repeat the fate of my friend. I don't want it. Please don't.

Ivan Ivanovich stood up and almost shouted, "No!"

The forest echoed it briefly: "No—no—no." And fell silent.

It was spring.

There were drops of the sky on the ground.

199

And it was so quiet.

So quiet, as if there were no evil anywhere.

But somewhere in the forest—a shot rang out! Three times! Who? Why? At what?

Perhaps a mean man had wounded that beautiful woodpecker and was finishing him off with two more shots.

Or perhaps a hunter had buried his dog, who was three years old.

No, there's no peace. Not even in this sky-blue temple with its columns of living oak, thought Ivan Ivanovich, standing in the forest, his white locks uncovered, his eyes turned heavenward. And it seemed like a spring prayer.

The forest was silent.